# ARRIVING AT A PLACE YOU'VE NEVER LEFT

# ARRIVING AT A PLACE YOU'VE NEVER LEFT

## LOIS RUBY

The Dial Press / New York

Library of Congress Cataloging in Publication Data
Ruby, Lois.
Arriving at a place you've never left.
Contents: Spring.—Faces at a dark window.—Justice.
—Heads, you go. Tales I stay.—Like a toy on the
end of a string. [etc.]
[1. Short stories] I. Title.
PZ7.R8314Ar   [Fic]   77-71521
ISBN 0-8037-0260-4

*Dedicated to*
*David, Ken, Jeff,*
*and especially Tom*

# CONTENTS

# ARRIVING AT A PLACE YOU'VE NEVER LEFT

# FACES AT A DARK WINDOW

Was it October, or November, when I first became aware of Mother's strange behavior? It's hard to remember exactly, because here in Houston all the months are so much alike. There are the hot ones, then the less hot ones, but who knows when it changes? Who knows when, exactly when, anything changes?

I came home from school one day. Oh, it was before Halloween. Of course. I couldn't forget Halloween. So it must have been October when I first noticed. Mother was sitting in the kitchen with a toothpick in her hand.

She was twirling it so gently, engrossed in its slow motion ballet.

"Mama?" She seemed not to hear me. I suppose she did, though, because she said, "Hello, Ellen," in such a faraway voice, and then she got up and went into the bathroom without ever looking my way.

Well, I thought, I must have really crossed her before I left for school that day. But I couldn't remember any particular incident. The morning was a usual one. She fixed us toast and hot chocolate, packed Alex's lunch, ran down to the dryer for some clean socks for him, refilled Daddy's coffee cup unconsciously, all the ordinary things that happen Monday through Friday at our house. No one talks much in the mornings. We're all either too sleepy or too busy getting our heads ready to meet the day outside. It would never occur to any of us to have a conversation over breakfast. Dinner time was when we all came to life as a family. Just as none of us spoke at breakfast, and no one expected Daddy to peek out from behind his newspaper, not one of us would have dreamed of bringing a paper to dinner.

When Alex had baseball, we all ate together at eight o'clock. If I had a rehearsal, we all ate at five. If Alex had baseball and I had a rehearsal on the same night, Daddy was furious. Daddy furious is one scary sight, so Alex and I usually worked it out between us: one time he missed baseball, and the next time I missed a rehearsal. It worked O.K. Anyway, Daddy was the only one in our family who was allowed to get mad.

Mother—well, now as I look back, I realize Mother was there and she wasn't. She ran our home pretty well. She always had good meals for us, got into most of our activities, encouraged us to bring friends home, and was usually neat and pleasant. Not exactly like Sandra's mother, who was a pal to us and used to play jacks with us when we were kids. But Mother was nice.

I guess Alex and I were so involved in our own lives that we never stopped to realize that Mother took part in nothing that did not have to do with us, and absolutely nothing with much vigor. It wasn't that she was dull. No, she read and could talk to us about things. But I don't think she had any real interests of her own, you know what I mean?

One day I asked, "Mama, do you feel exploited?"

"Ellen! Where would you come up with such an idea?"

"Oh, you know feminism and all. Don't you wish you were more liberated?"

She gave it a moment's thought, as though she'd been hearing about women's lib, but it had to do with people of some other sex, not her own.

"What would I have to be liberated from?" She thought a good long moment more, then added, "Freedom's in a person's mind, that's all."

I accepted that. I was on the personal-freedom trip

right then, and into existentialism, which I could pro-
nounce, but never quite knew the meaning of. So it
seemed like a really meaty answer to me.

Last week I thought over the whole conversation and
the mood that went along with it that day, and it began
to occur to me that Mother really had told me a lot
more than I could hear then. Her mind was getting
away from her, losing its freedom, or getting too much
freedom, I'm not sure which.

Anyway, one day I brought home someone from my
trig class, a girl named Greta. I didn't know her very
well. I didn't know trig very well either, which is why
I brought Greta the Slide Rule home with me. As we
opened the door, I could just tell something was wrong.
Did I smell it? Feel it? How could I have known?
Everything looked like it should, neat but lived in.
I noticed that the gigantic rubber plant by the door was
kind of dry, but often Mother forgets to water it. She
says it's a wonder she remembers to water her kids
regularly.

The Slide Rule and I went into the kitchen, because
of course we were starved, and there were the breakfast dishes all over the table. The hot chocolate pot had
a hole burned through it, because the burner under it
was still on low. I was really embarrassed, and I started
rushing around to tidy up. Then I thought, something
must have happened to Alex that Mother left so sud-

denly, or to Mother. I dashed into her room, and this,
I swear, is just how I found her:

She was in an orange quilted robe, rhythmically
swaying in her swivel rocker. Her robe was soaked.
Her eyes looked empty. There were streaks down her
face where tears had been.

"Mama? What's wrong?" I ran to her and put my
arms around her shoulders, but she didn't smell too in-
viting, so I backed away.

As though nothing unusual had happened, she
smiled and said, "Did you have a nice day at school?"
Then she got up, noticed the condition of her robe,
and said in a comfortable way, "Goodness, I must
attend to things!"

I couldn't think of anything to say, especially when
I saw old Slide Rule standing at the door with eyes
like question marks. I mumbled something about
Mother not feeling on top of things today, and we'd
get to trig some other time, and Greta took the hint,
thank God, and left.

I cut trig the rest of the week.

I decided not to tell anyone what had happened, not
even Mother. Besides, she seemed her old self right
after her shower that afternoon, and I don't think she
even remembered.

One day it hit me. Menopause! Mother was already
thirty when I was born, so she could be at the age. And

I'd heard that lots of women had weird experiences with it. I felt so much better that I stopped on the way home and bought her a cinnamon-colored carnation at Safeway, and we both had a good old-fashioned cry over the flower.

Then came Halloween.

It's really hard to be sixteen on Halloween. You're enough of a kid to almost wish you could dress up in a costume that would really knock everybody out. On the other hand, you're pretty adult, and you can see how dumb all those skeletons and witches and home-made, fat pumpkins are. So you stay home and pass out candy. Which is what I was going to do that year.

Alex was a pirate, and for his costume we used most of what he wore last year to be a hobo, plus a gold earring. We had an early dinner, since the small kids would be coming about six thirty. It's kind of like turning a radio on and off at our house. You turn a switch and everybody jabbers and chatters all through dinner. Turn the switch again and it's all over. Daddy goes into the den to read the evening paper. Mother sighs and clears the table. Alex carries a few dishes to the sink, then settles down by the TV with his school books open. And I, well, it's hard to pin down exactly what I do night after night. Anyway, we're all pretty quiet after dinner, except for the clunking and clink-ing of dishes and the television on, turned down low.

But on Halloween, everything was different. Oh,

Daddy was in the den with his paper, as usual. I really wondered every night how much could have happened in the world since he'd devoured the morning paper. On Halloween, Mother wasn't worrying about the dishes, and the TV wasn't on, and Alex and I were pretty noisy. You can't get a pirate into his costume quietly.

"Ellen, get outta here while I get my pirate pants on."

"Oh, brother, nine years old and you think you'll shock me in your little jockey shorts?" But I left, since I needed to get the make-up for his face anyway. Mother was going through her jewelry to find a good cheap gold earring. When Alex was decent again, I went back into his room.

"Alex, get your mug over here into the light so I can make you even uglier."

"I'll never be as ugly as you."

"You already are."

"Hah! You admitted you're ugly." I socked him one in the ribs for that, not too hard. I was very generous with the black eye liner and smudge stuff, and I gave him a pair of eyebrows like you wouldn't believe. That's what Halloween's for, isn't it? Then we made a fake peg leg and tied a scarf around his head, and I have to say, he looked fierce.

Mother came in then with the earring. She stopped at the door suddenly, then her face turned to paste. For a minute I was afraid she was going to faint.

"Hey, Mom, really scared you, didn't I?" said Long John. But Mother said nothing. Her hands were shaking so much that the earring fell to the floor and made what seemed like a terrific noise. Alex picked it up, watching Mother the whole time.

"Mom? You O.K.?" By then she was shaking all over, and we both led her over to the bed. Alex looked really scared. A kid never expects his mother to weaken like that. I was sort of getting used to it. But then, I'm seven years older than my brother.

Mother lay rigidly on the bed, her hands fluttering around her face as though they were surprised they belonged to the same person.

"Alex, go get Daddy."

Finally she said something. "He . . . gave me such a start," she whispered, her voice so wobbly.

"Alex?"

"Alex? Oh, yes, it was Alex. Oh, yes." She began to sit up, but I made her lie back.

"Rest, Mama. Alex is bringing Daddy."

Her eyebrows became upside down V's, and she bolted up. "No, don't call him in here." Daddy, however, was at the door, the newspaper trailing behind him.

"What is it, Anna?"

"Nothing. I'm fine. They got upset for nothing."

"Well, my God, Alex came tearing into the den like

your hair was on fire. Glad to see you're O.K." His mind was already back to some article on page nine or something. "Those blasted kids will be ringing this doorbell every two seconds pretty soon. I'm going into the bathroom to finish my paper."

When Daddy left, Mother sank back down into the pillow.

"Jeeze, Mom, you scared me out of my skin," Alex said, adjusting his peg leg.

"Why? What did I do—exactly?"

"What did you do? Gol-lee, did you forget already?" Alex gave me the old crazy sign with the twirling finger, while Mother stared at the airplane hanging from the ceiling. Suddenly, she stood up.

"Why are you two making such a big fuss? I only got a bit frightened with seeing—Alex dressed up like that." She said "Alex" as though she'd only heard the name once or twice before.

"Well, Ellen's the one who told me to get Dad. I didn't get excited. I mean, gol-lee, it's Halloween."

Mother looked at me with a slight flicker of recognition in her tired eyes. "Ellen," she said, then "Ellen" again, as though she were trying the name on.

Well, I don't mind telling you, I was shaken. The only thing I could think to do was leave the room. Alex followed me, and he seemed glad to do it, too. We both felt pretty relieved to be away from her.

The doorbell was ringing, and Alex was looking for

a paper bag worthy—that is, big enough—to hold all the junk he was planning to collect, and we were so busy that we let Mother slip from our thoughts.

Just as the Sylvesters' two little brats came to the door dressed as a cat and a mouse, Mother came out of Alex's room and walked, as if she were on a tightrope, to the front door.

"Hi, Mrs. Abel," the girls said. "Are you going trick-'r-treating too?" they asked, running off down the driveway. I could see why they thought so. She was a horror. She had smeared her face in patches with black eye shadow, then drawn lips way above and below her own in bright red. Her eyes were tiny dark spots lost in rings and rings of black eye liner. Worst of all, she'd opened her blouse and you could see where she'd drawn thick black lines down her neck and chest.

"Mother," screamed Alex, "what the heck are you doing dressed up like that?" He swallowed, staring at her. "You really freaked me out!" He was trying to see the humor in her disguise, but he was blinking fast to hold back the tears. I couldn't tell whether he was embarrassed, or just plain scared. As for me, I couldn't do a thing but stare, especially when she started out the door like that.

"Mama, come back in." I ran after her, but she squirmed out of my reach and walked in a daze down our driveway. I watched, horrified, as she bumped into costumed kids like they weren't even there, then headed straight for the street. A car, thank God, was watching out for trick-or-treaters, and it just missed her. She never saw it.

"Ellen, I think she's flipped out," Alex told me. We rushed after her and pulled her back toward our driveway, but our touch made her absolutely wild, and she started screaming and shouting and fighting us off, until all three of us were on the ground.

"Get your hands off me. Goddamn it, get your hands off me. Leave me alone. Both of you go to hell and leave me alone," she screamed. Mother didn't usually say things like that around us.

As you can imagine, quite a crowd was forming, and while I was out of my head with fright, mostly I was embarrassed beyond belief. How could this be happening to my mother, to me?

When she fainted, somebody's father carried her into our living room, and as I watched her lie there on the sofa, all I felt, I'm ashamed to say, was a great revulsion for my mother.

Twice a month, on Sundays, we visit her. She didn't recognize us the first few times, and after the third visit we all decided Alex shouldn't go anymore. I guess he always felt a little closer to Mother than I did. He looks a lot like her. I guess that's why it tore him up so much to visit her.

As for me, I have to tell you honestly, I was angry

that she would do such a thing to me, and if there was any love that I felt, it sure hid itself well. After six or seven visits, I began to find the whole thing kind of fascinating, as though I had private access to somebody's case files. Not my mother's.

Then on the eighth visit, something changed. Daddy usually said his hello in a friendly way, asked after her comfort, then just settled down in a chair for the rest of the time. It really wasn't easy to make conversation, and sometimes all three of us had long periods of silence that made me nervous.

But that day, on the eighth visit, Mother seemed not as quiet as we'd been used to seeing her. Before, she'd moved and talked very slowly, very quietly, when she talked at all. But that day her eyes seemed more awake, and she looked like she was waiting for us to say something.

"Mama, we're doing *Death of a Salesman* next month, and I'm stage-managing it almost myself."

"I . . . read . . . the play . . . once."

Daddy sat up. He hadn't expected Mother to respond.

"It's very . . . sad."

"I cried the first time I read it, Mama."

"Very sad."

"Mama, do you cry much now?"

"I'm not sure."

Well, I was a living example of crying by that point.

I cry easily anyway. Mother seemed to be trying so hard to concentrate on me, really trying to look deeply into my face. She kept blinking to clear the blur away.

"Ellen, it's been so long. I've . . . been alone . . . so long."

Daddy's voice startled me. "We were here two Sundays ago, Anna."

She paid no attention to him. She seemed so frightened, like she was in a cold, dark cave and couldn't find her way out. I did something that doesn't come too easily for me, especially considering the way I'd been feeling about my mother the past few months. I reached out for her hand, even though what came to my mind was how she smelled that day Greta was over. She grabbed me with a ferocity that surprised me at first and then made me feel very grown up all of a sudden. Here I was, her child, leading her as she'd led me through the crowds at the downtown department stores when I was small.

She finally cried, and Daddy wasn't sure whether to call for the doctor or to wait and see if things got worse. He was fidgeting uneasily with some rubber bands he took out of his coat pocket.

"I will make it, won't I, Ellen?"

"Sure, Mama, you will."

"I'm so afraid. It's terrifying to be alone in here." She pointed, as if she meant inside herself. "But you are here, so I can't be too lost, can I?"

I was bewildered myself, but I assured her, "No, Mama."

"I'm so tired," she said, and her eyes drifted shut. Daddy took the cue immediately and gratefully.

"Well, we'll go then, Anna. If you need anything tell Dr. Roget and we'll send it right along to you. Don't worry about a thing." He gave her a fatherly kiss, the kind he usually gave me when I was going to stay the night at a friend's. Then he opened the door. Mother did not respond to him in any way.

"Good-bye, Mama. I'm so happy to see you're much better today."

She attempted a smile, but it broke as it was forming. I had almost closed the door behind me when I heard her faint voice.

"Ellen, tell . . . Alex, please?"

"Oh, yes, Mama, I will." My voice sounded thick with tears. "I'll tell Alex for you, Mama, as soon as we get home."

# FOUND BY A LOST
# CHILD

"Hey, Shana, me and the guys are going down to the lake. Wanna come?"

"Which guys?"

"You know, the usual."

"You don't need me along."

"What're you talking about? You're the only real live female we got. Come on."

"David, I need to talk to you."

"Sure. We can talk on the way."

"No, I mean really talk."

"Well, what do you expect me to do with Nat and Alan?"

"Oh, they probably could get along without you for ten or fifteen minutes. It might be hard, but they could do it."

"Yeah, I guess we can shake them when we get out to the lake," he said dubiously.

"Listen, if this isn't convenient for you, I'll call your secretary for an appointment in the morning."

"You don't have to get sarcastic."

"I'm just asking for a little time alone with you, David."

"O.K., O.K. Pick you up in about half an hour."

Shana put down the receiver carefully. "That was David," she told her mother, who was typing near the phone. She turned off the typewriter and watched her daughter pace the narrow width of the room.

"You'll be relieved when it's done, Shane. Are you sure you don't want me with you when you talk to him?"

"No, Mother. I've got to handle this myself."

"I'll be home all evening, Shane, if you need me." She gave her daughter an encouraging smile, unreturned by the girl, who was too anxious to notice it.

Elaine Miller, with her model-like appearance and chic hair style, looked more the elder sister than the mother. Perhaps it was because Shana was born when she herself was only seventeen that Elaine was able to empathize so fully with her daughter. She turned the typewriter back on as Shana retied the knot of shirt at her waist, untied it again, and finally threw the shirt on a chair. A sweatshirt would do better, she decided.

David drove a World War II ambulance, and as it sputtered and shook its way up Shana's driveway, doors began opening and bodies tumbling out.

"Ready, guys? David? Alan? Hit it!"

"SHAA-NAH!" In unison they bellowed out her name. The deep opera voice in the crowd belonged to Alan Fortune, a tall guy with thick glasses and thin hair. He was uncomfortable around girls, but he didn't think of Shana that way. She was more like a friend, so she was safe. But, then, he had unusual taste. He preferred Rachmaninoff to Elton John and milk to Coke. He had a vegetable garden that was of keen importance to him, since he ate no meat. David kept him around because he was amused by Alan's fussiness. To his face David called him "The Old Maid" and behind his back, "The Virgin."

Nat Goren backed into the ambulance and played a solo on the horn. Whereas Alan seemed unaware of the special qualities of girls, Nat was obsessed with them. He never stopped drooling over girls or speculating about their real or imagined potential. He bragged a lot, though his successes, so far, were severely limited. It wasn't that he was undesirable. He just had an unmarketable personality. He was always playing Bogie's famous movie parts and talking about horoscopes and ear staples and dogs with ESP. One girl, Doris Bandowsky, liked dogs well enough apparently, because she went out with Nat three or four times. Then she came down with hepatitis and was out of circulation. And the thought of all that liver made Nat feel yellow all over, which turned him off. There went a great romance. That left Nat to hang around with Alan, and the two hung around David, and David had Shana, so it turned out to be the four of them quite often.

Shana ran out of the house, smiling at the untidy crew that had come to pick her up. But her eyes fell uneasily on David, which he saw, and he kissed her lightly. Then they all four squeezed into the front seat of the ambulance. Nobody ever sat in the back if they could help it, although when Nat and Alan weren't along, things were different.

David blew the horn as they approached the lake, a common courtesy to lake-shore lovers. Then he yelled, "Up, everybody. I want to see all your feet on the floor." Heads popped up in several cars, then disappeared again.

"Hey, you two going skinny-dipping tonight?" asked Nat, tumbling out onto the sand.

"Not a chance. We wouldn't give you guys that much of a skin show for free," David answered. He threw a little sand in Alan's face. It gave him some kind of terrific feeling to be the only guy with a girl friend, and he loved being enviable. Not that Shana was exactly Raquel Welch. Her body was O.K., a little thick here and there. Voluptuous, Nat said. Her face was ordinary; it had the usual fixtures, but nicely arranged. She hardly ever got zits. Her teeth weren't too straight, though. Her hair, that was the thing. It was so full and red, and it shone and fell all over her face and neck and back when she moved anything at all. She must have washed it about five times a week, it was so shiny.

"David," Shana whispered. "We have to talk."

"Hey, what's bugging you? We're here for fun, right? Don't look so grim."

"Romeo and Juliet, quit your whispering. You're making me horny," Nat yelled from further down the beach. He and Alan were building sand castles in obscene mounds.

"David, I mean it."

David Frankel was not a person who got serious easily. "Aw, Shana, you always want to have a discussion. You don't need a boy friend, you need a panel moderator. Call up David Brinkley for a date some night, huh?"

"David." Her tone suggested he'd better sober up.

"What is it?" He was digging his bare toes into the sand.

"David, I'm pregnant."

For a long time he said nothing. She was wondering if he'd heard, until finally he replied, "Did a doctor tell you for sure?"

"Yes. It's for sure."

"Jesus, Shana." He felt like his stomach had dropped out. "Jesus, how could you?"

"Oh, it was simple. I sent away for it by mail order." She felt her face go hot with anger.

"Is this a joke?"

"I laugh about it night and day, especially when I'm throwing up."

"What are you going to do?"

"I don't know."

"What choices do you have?"

"Well, I could kill myself. That's one."

"Be serious."

"I would, if you'd let me."

"Hey, Nat, take the wagon home, will you? Shana and I have something we gotta talk about."

"You say something, Frankel?"

"Take the meat wagon home," he yelled back up the beach. "Shana and I will walk."

Nat and Alan were accustomed to taking orders from David, so they left immediately.

"What are you planning to do. You planning to—?"

"Get rid of it?"

"Yeah," he agreed, with a sigh of relief.

"I don't know."

"Well, you gotta do something." He walked a couple of steps ahead of Shana. A breeze blew in the small distance between them, and Shana wrapped her arms around one another for warmth.

"Hell, you don't want to—have it, do you?"

"David, I just don't know."

"Well, you better make up your mind. How long's it been?"

"Maybe two months."

"Oh, Jesus!" He spun around with a sudden inspiration. "Sometimes girls lose them. What do you call it? Miscarry. Maybe that will happen to you—if you're lucky."

Shana shook her head. "You can't count on that."

"Well, Jesus, Shana, what are you going to do?"

"Listen to yourself, David. You keep asking me what am *I* going to do. What about you? You're in this as much as I am, you know."

David stopped walking, and when Shana caught up to him, she saw a curious look in his eyes. His face hinted that it was the first time he'd considered that he was really involved. He was inspecting every corner of that idea. He was in it as much as she? He tentatively reached out to touch her arm, but she inched away. It was so imperceptible, it might not have happened at all. He came to a decision quickly. "You'll get rid of it. I'll help out any way I can. I've got some bread put away."

Shana felt chills crawl up her back, and her reaction was immediate and firm. "I'm going to have it."

"What? Two minutes ago you didn't know what you were going to do."

"Now I'm sure."

He gave her a patronizing look, eyes half-closed. "O.K., listen." He spoke as though she were a five-year-old needing directions on how to get home from the playground. "Tomorrow you ask the doctor where to go—in town, or to New York, or wherever. I'll go to the bank and get the money. A week from now it'll all be over, and we can go back to our normal life. See?"

Her voice was unyielding. "You can, David, but I can't. There's something living in me, and I can't just rub it out."

"Since when are you the big moralist, the Reverend Miller?"

"Since it became obvious how little you care about life."

"I care about life. My own, yours. That's the important thing. That thing you say is in you, that's not a life, it's a ball of cells, a thing."

"I'm going to do it, David. I'm having the—baby."

Baby. It was the first time the word had been mentioned. Baby. Baby. It was as though one of them had thrown a stone into the lake, and the circles were shimmering and widening and echoing the word: Baby.

"You know what this sounds like to me? Like you're doing this just to spite me, to get your hooks in me or something. I'm not falling for it."

"That's not it, David. I just know now that I can't get rid of it. Maybe yesterday I could have. Not today."

"What the hell's so different about today?"

"You've made it all seem a lot clearer," she said, sharply.

"Jesus, what are you doing to us? Look"—he grabbed both her elbows—"it could be so simple, and safe, safe for you. Everything could be all right again, afterward."

"It'll never be all right again, David. No, I've made up my mind."

He dropped her elbows in anger. "Hold it. You said we were both in this together, right? Well, I say get rid of it. I don't want a kid. You don't want a kid. Get rid of it."

Sounding a little like a spoiled child, she answered, "It's my body, and I guess I'll just have to decide on my own. So you stay out of it."

"Shana, Jesus, we're sixteen. How could you screw up our lives this way?"

"Crummy choice of words, David."

A horrible thought struck him. "You're not expecting me to marry you, are you?"

Shana pulled her hair off to one side and combed it with her fingers. "I'm expecting nothing from you,

David. I take it back. We're not in this together. Just forget it."

"Forget it? First you drop a bomb on me, total me, then you tell me to forget it?"

"You will," she sighed, and she walked quickly up to the road.

David started after her, but he knew that she had no intention of letting him near her. And maybe if she walked a couple of miles, it would take care of things naturally. Besides, he needed to be alone. He had a weighty problem to think through—forget it, she said —and he was unaccustomed to the exercise.

Elaine Miller waited anxiously for her daughter. She had prayed that it would go well with David. Hadn't he been on top of things when Shana broke her arm in the volleyball game out at the lake? He'd kept his head, hadn't he? Driven her to the emergency room, called home? And when Shana lost the student-body election, he was a great help, joking her out of her dejection and taking her out for pizza to celebrate her defeat. He was O.K.—but not up to this, not something this big. As soon as Shana opened the door, Elaine knew.

Shana wasn't crying, but her voice was thin with sadness. "I told him I'm having the baby."

"It's your decision, Shana. We'll work it out."

"It has nothing to do with him anymore."

"I know."

"Oh, Mother."

"We can handle it, Shane. Do you want to keep the baby?"

"No."

Elaine nodded. "We'll talk to Dr. Hershey in the morning. She'll tell us how to go about making all the arrangements."

"Yes, Mother." The two had their arms around each other like weary boxers.

Elaine was having a flashback: same scene, different room, and her own mother saying, "She's just a child herself."

Nat and Alan threw rocks at the window until Shana peered out.

"Hey, Chubs, we're going bowling. Want to come?"

"I'll be right down," she called to them. She thought for a moment about how she used to ask her mother's permission all the time. Now it seemed kind of ridiculous to do that. Anyway, Elaine was away at a convention. Before, she would never have left Shana alone. Shana would have stayed with her grandmother or a friend. That seemed kind of ridiculous now too.

Nat and Alan and Shana had been together a lot in the last few months. While no one said much about David, Alan and Nat felt responsible for Shana in his absence.

Shana gracelessly piled into the front seat of Nat's

1956 Cadillac, next to Nat, and Alan slid in beside her. She rearranged the load in her lap so that she could breathe more easily. Lately the baby was taking up so much room that there wasn't much left over for her. But, she thought, it'll be all over within a month.

"So, are you feeling O.K.?" Alan was the more paternal of the two.

"Oh, fat, but O.K. Guess what."

"What's that?"

"I've lost my navel."

Nat pulled the car to a screeching halt, threw it into park, and jumped out.

"What are you doing, you idiot?" asked Shana.

"I'm looking for your navel. It's got to be here somewhere."

"Get back in the car," she squealed, laughing until the muscles in her abdomen were sore from the effort. The baby kicked all the while, as though he/she were enjoying it as well. "You guys are totally bananas. You're the best friends a girl could have. And in my condition, I need all the friends I can get. That reminds me, how's your friend David?"

The boys stopped smiling. They still saw David; they couldn't help it. It was as if he held them, somehow. But things were different. They were all different, except maybe for David.

"He's O.K. Into the track season." That was Alan's

way of explaining why Shana never saw David. Shana, of course, understood why.

"He's making tracks to get away from me, you mean."

"Come on, Shana," Alan gently prodded.

"No, it's all right. I used to be really bitter about it, you remember. But now I know that David and I never really loved each other. Not truly. This"—she patted her belly—"only quickened what would have happened anyway."

"Yeah, but he could've—" Nat began weakly.

"I don't care anymore, Nat."

Nat glanced at her sideways to verify that, then back to the road. Maybe she really didn't care. "Well, we'll give the dudes at the bowling alley some kicks when this pregnant chick hits the lanes," he said, speeding up.

"Yeah, everyone will think I swallowed my bowling ball!"

Wherever they went, people stared. The first thing they noticed, or so Shana thought, was that she didn't have a wedding ring on. Then they looked from Nat's face to Alan's, to guess which one was the father. When the faces offered no definitive proof, people seemed to zero in below the waists of the two boys, as though they could tell that way, and then they glanced incredulously at the strange trio. At first Shana was terribly self-conscious about it, but after a couple of months it occurred to her that it must be as difficult for the boys as for her. After all, just by being with her in public they were as much as taking responsibility for her state and providing more gossip for speculators than if one were with her alone. In time, Shana found herself almost amused by the public curiosity and genuinely touched by the fact that the boys never seemed to notice the looks and whispers of people around them. Tonight, Shana felt, the bowling alley was overstuffed with inquiring eyes.

"You guys mind if I don't bowl tonight?"

Alan glanced sharply at her face. "You O.K.?"

"Yes, sure, but it's getting harder and harder to bend over. And my back sort of, you know—no, you wouldn't know—just kind of hurts."

"Well, you can still bend over the score sheet, can't you? Me and Alan will give you some professional display here tonight. Ready?"

But she didn't hear him. A strange thing was happening inside her body. Like someone had lifted the whole middle section up about six inches, then gently set it down again.

"Hey, Shana. Where are you?" Nat asked, waving his hand in front of her eyes. "Alan rolled a strike, man. The only one he'll get all night, and you missed it."

"Oh, sorry." She filled in the little square, her other hand pushing gently on her back. The little bit of pressure made it feel more comfortable.

"Hey, Dick Weber, what are you going to do with that seven-ten split?" Alan asked.

"Split, man."

"I would if I were you. You'll never make it, unless you have a very fat ball," Alan warned.

"Oh, yeah? Watch this." He let the ball go and watched it smoothly roll straight down the center, nowhere near either pin.

Shana teased, "Too bad, Nathaniel," as Nat sank onto the bench.

Then Shana felt her abdomen rise again, hang there for a few seconds, and slowly amble back down. "This is new," she said, hardly realizing she spoke.

"What's that?"

"I think the baby's trying to stand up," she giggled. But just the same, she wondered. It happened a couple of more times, just like that, and it felt curious but not unpleasant. There were so many movements in her body these days, movements with which she'd come to an uneasy peace. She stood up to change positions, and as she did so she felt a trickle of water running down each leg, then a gush. Quickly she sat down, in a puddle.

"Oh, mercy," she cried.

"Shana? What is it?" Alan's face was white.

Shana was wiping tears off her face with the back of her sleeve. But they kept coming, and the water too. Nat was right there, embarrassed to look too closely into her face. Tears made him feel awkward.

"Nat, Alan, I think the baby's coming."

"Your mother. We'll call your mother." Alan fumbled in his pocket for a dime.

"No, Mother's in Pittsburgh," Shana cried. It wasn't supposed to happen for nearly a month. Not for another month. "Oh, Alan, what do I do?"

"Now don't worry. Don't worry. What's your doctor's name? I'll call her," Alan said. Nat guided Shana over to the bench, as though the brittle cold plastic might be a more comfortable place for her. Actually, he didn't want to just stand there doing nothing.

Shana was so wet she hardly noticed what she was sitting on anyway. Then a rumbling rose in her again, a mild volcano, but enough to assure her that there was no way to turn it off now.

Alan ran back to them. "Dr. Hershey says to take her over to Methodist Hospital. She'll meet us there."

Things had subsided for the moment, and Shana clearly heard the "us." Absently she wondered where David was, but the thought didn't linger.

Nat drove as fast as he dared, over curbs, around a motorcycle, through three yellow lights, glancing nervously at Shana whenever he could.

All the reading she'd done, all the talks with Dr. Hershey, the classes she'd taken, the reassurances from her mother—all these had prepared her for what she was about to do. And yet the experience was still unknown, still frightening. What she felt more strongly still, mounting with each contraction, was a flush of excitement. The closest she'd ever come to feeling this way was when she was thirteen and meeting her father for the first time. But this was different. This was all her own personal adventure, not a feeling to mirror or to measure by the response in someone else's face.

They pulled up to the emergency entrance and Alan helped her out while Nat parked the car. It did not occur to either of them to go into the emergency room without Nat. So they waited.

The three of them approached the admitting nurse. "Yes?"

"I'm going to have a baby."

"How grand," she said, not looking up from her mountain of papers. Finally she did glance up, looking from Alan's face to Nat's and back to Shana's, splotched with tears and excitement. "Well, which one of you is the father?"

"I am," they both responded.

"You're doing beautifully, Shana. You're almost to the end. One or two more big pushes and it will all be over." Dr. Hershey had carefully avoided saying anything about the baby. Instead she focused on Shana and her strength and her hard work to release her body's burden.

Shana had never worked so hard in all her life.

Every muscle strained: her throat, her neck, her arms pulling on the restraints, her chest pushing down on the load—she could feel her heart thumping as she held her breath—her abdomen, her uterus, the birth canal throbbing with the impact of a being trying to push its way through an incredibly narrow alley.

"O.K. now, Shana. Relax. Take a deep breath. Let it out. Another one. Let it out. Another one, hold it, pull up, and push as hard as you can. Fine, Shana, fine."

Her head pounded with the strain, and she thought her throat would burst. Then it happened. A marvelous feeling of relief as her abdomen collapsed and the head was out. The rest Dr. Hershey handled herself, for Shana was lost somewhere else.

It was a strange mixture of feelings: euphoria; exhilaration that her body had worked so well for her; pride that she'd done something momentous, for if the accomplishment were not momentous, how could it possibly have cost so much effort? She felt a physical relief that the heavy load she'd borne for many months was gone. There were tears in her eyes and again her throat swelled. The ordeal was over. Her body was her own again, no longer host to someone else.

Suddenly Shana felt all the exhaustion that had been building for these many hours, and she dropped off to sleep. She was surprised to find that she had been asleep when they woke her minutes later to take her to her room.

They all look alike, he thought, passing the nursery. Ugly and wrinkled and bald. David was scanning the numbers above the doors, looking for Shana's room. He hadn't decided what to say to her. For the first time he could remember, he wished he were taller. He felt conscious of the fact that he was only seventeen, rather small for his age. Maybe he should have worn a tie. He felt very uncomfortable with the hospital smells. He knocked on her door, the furthest from the nursery.

"Come in," a quiet voice called. Shana was half sitting up in bed, swallowed by her hospital gown. There was another bed in the room, but it was empty and the shades were drawn next to it. She probably hadn't expected David, but neither did she seem surprised to see him.

"I thought I'd stop by."

"You didn't have to."

"Well, I've been thinking about you."

"Why?"

David sighed. Whatever made him think he had loved her? She was always bitchy, always making him feel she was better than he was. "The guys told me about it."

Shana nodded lightly.

"You look great."

"I look awful."

She could never take a compliment either. Always

turned it around and made him feel dumb for saying it. "No, really." He walked around to the other side of the bed, the darker side. "I guess you must hate me."

"Not really."

"Maybe not, but you're sure giving off hostile vibes."

"You're feeling what you expect to feel, David."

It was that superior Dr. Sigmund Freud tone she used on him sometimes. "Well, I guess you have reason to hate me."

Shana shrugged her shoulders. "If it'll make you feel any better."

David looked around the room, hoping for a cue. "Your mother O.K.?"

"Fine, fine."

"You're sure lucky to be missing school."

Shana motioned toward a stack of books on her bedside table. "Mr. Glazer and Mrs. Rigetti took care of that."

"Oh, yeah, you can always count on them." He glanced around the room again. "Listen, you could probably read better if I opened the drapes for you." He started toward the window.

"No, I like it this way."

"Yeah, sure." It was so stuffy in the room. "Hey"— he backed toward the door. Why did she have to keep the drapes shut? He needed air—"hey, if there's anything you need—"

"O.K." She closed her eyes. She was still awfully tired and had been finding herself dozing on and off since the delivery.

"I'll call you when you get home, O.K.?" he asked from the door. But she had fallen asleep and didn't hear him.

David passed by the nursery on the way to the elevator. On an impulse motivated by—what? obligation? curiosity?—he searched the name cards trying to locate the baby.

A nurse, sensitive to the eyes of nervous new fathers, saw when he found the name he was looking for, and she moved the cradle over to the window. At first David drew back and wanted to walk right off to the elevator behind him. But he was held against his will, fascinated.

The baby was bundled in a pink blanket. Is it a girl, he wondered? They must wrap the girls in pink. Her head was turned in David's direction, compliments of the nurse, and she seemed at once so pink and so blue, with veins everywhere. She slept with one unbelievably small finger over her nose, and she made sucking movements with her lips.

Could it be, he thought, that this baby came from me? A curious feeling of awe mixed with revulsion at so disturbing a thought came over him. *I am part of that? That, she, is part of me?* His chest felt very tight, and for a second he thought his knees might not hold him up. It was an unfamiliar intensity he felt as he stared at the peacefully sleeping bundle.

The elevator door opened, but he didn't hear it. A couple in their early thirties approached. They were laughing and holding hands, so caught up in themselves and each other that they didn't notice the boy by the nursery window, but neither did he see them.

All at once the woman squealed in pleasure. "Eric, look! They have our baby right in front for us. Oh, isn't she absolutely gorgeous?"

The man called Eric was busy snapping his fingers to wake the baby up, as if she could hear him through the thick nursery glass.

"Can you believe it? Our own little girl at last. Who do you think they'll say she looks like, you or me?" Their eyes glowed with the joy and wonder of the first days of parenthood.

David took his eyes off the baby and saw them for the first time. He had a sudden flash of understanding, then quickly moved toward the waiting elevator. Immediately the door slid shut, leaving him alone, inside.

# HEADS YOU GO,
# TAILS I STAY

Zeke always felt good and lazy on Saturday afternoons. The house was as noisy as a zoo just before feeding time, with Rita mooning around on the phone, and Jonathan practicing his trombone, and Jenny throwing wooden blocks, or throwing up, and George Q. building a fort on the third-floor stairway, and the hammering, and the shouting that took the place of an intercom, and Ernie's squeaky tricycle in the backyard. But, then, Zeke didn't stay home for the peace and quiet. He was there so he could lie around and do some reading, with the noise and confusion he was used to for proper digesting of important stuff. Today *Playboy,* tomorrow the world was his general philosophy. On a Saturday afternoon in April, you just can't get into anything too heavy. Not with the windows all open around the attic room and a furry breeze tickling you. No, it was definitely a *Playboy* afternoon.

Ruthie Bellini drove up on page thirty-seven. As she pulled into the driveway, Zeke yelled down to her, "Hey, Bellini."

She leaned out the car window. "Zeke? That's got to be you up there. Listen, you could call me by my first name, you know, as if I were a girl."

"A girl? Naw. Couldn't be. You're my sister's friend. That makes you a neuter."

"Thanks a lot, Cassidy."

"Come on up. My room's a mess."

"I feel a little dumb yelling up to a voice I can't see a head attached to. At least you could look out the window when you invite me up."

He poked a grinning face out the window.

"Yukk. Put your head back in."

"What are you talking about? I'm gorgeous."

"Oh, sure, if you like freaks," she replied, running up the steps into the Cassidys' ancient brick house.

The front door was open, as usual. Most often there was a dog or a few cats or an escaped gerbil in the hallway. If there were a huge brown rat, or even an elephant there, no one would have gotten too excited. They were a remarkably calm and together bunch, these Cassidys, considering the size of the menagerie.

The smallest Cassidy, nearly a year old, was parading in a very large, homemade playpen in front of the door, surveying all passersby. Her eyes scrunched up when Ruthie entered, wondering if the giant in the doorway knew the secret password. The password, of course, was Jenny.

"Hi, Jenny. Rita home?"

"Beh deh babababab mmn."

"Oh? And what else is new?" But Jenny had lost interest in the conversation and was watching a bird perched on the bannister outside.

"Anybody home?" shouted Ruthie. "Rita?"

"Who is that?" a nasal voice called from the kitchen. The door below the stairs swung open for Mrs. Cassidy. She was wiping her hands on her apron, then behind her to make sure. She was a round little woman, joyfully devoted to her family but a bit tired-looking from too many of them. A few years before, she had decided that since there were only a certain number of hours in the day, and a gargantuan number of things to do in that day to keep a family of four (now six) children and one highly energetic husband content, she would have to sacrifice something. She gleefully settled upon housework as her sacrifice, and her house was never seen totally clean after that.

No one objected. When official company was due, the family organized a labor gang and set the house in order in something under fifty-five minutes. Still, there was always one room off limits to outsiders, where clothes discovered after the hanging brigade were tossed, where the vacuum was pushed and the door pulled shut just as the company was banging the rusted old knocker on the front door.

"Oh, Ruthie, hi. Rita's, well, I wonder where she is. Is Jenny wet? Did you notice on the way in?" She was already at the playpen, her hand automatically reaching around the corners of Jenny's diaper. "She's good for another hour or so. At least till I show you what's happening in the kitchen. George Q.," she yelled, "get this bike out of the living room." George Q. (Q for Quinion, Mrs. Cassidy's favorite granduncle) came tumbling down the stairs in the special haphazard way of a seven-year-old.

"Gee, Mom, I guess ya want it to rust outside, huh? You want it to get corrupted?"

"Corroded, and it won't, not if you put it in the garage." George Q. reluctantly wheeled it out the front door. Ruthie noticed a dirty wheel mark along the bicycle route, but Mrs. Cassidy didn't seem to see it, or if she did, it didn't matter.

"You're just in time to see Hector's pups. She just foaled yesterday. I guess you don't use 'foaled' for dogs. Oh, well. What a mess. Bloody puppies everywhere,

and her throwing up. Come on, look at the kitchen."
The kitchen was a jungle of plaster, buckets, tools, wallpaper rolled up, and all of them surrounding Mr. Cassidy. For recreation he was remodeling the kitchen,
while in another corner of the gigantic room Mrs.
Cassidy was returning to a huge bowl which she began
stirring furiously with a long wooden spoon. Her lips
counted the stirs.

"Well, Ruthie. Come. Put on some overalls and make
yourself useful."

"I don't think I'd be too useful, Mr. Cassidy," she
said, stepping over a Campbell's tomato soup can of
nails. "I'd probably plaster myself onto the wall."

"Can't be done, can't be done," Mr. Cassidy sang.
He was a giant among a family of dwarfs, maybe six
feet three. None of the children seemed to have in-
herited his height. He was about the busiest man
Ruthie knew. He was a carpenter all day, ran a small
TV repair business on the side, and kept his ample
family stocked in bookcases and shelves and most of the
furniture they used. In his spare time, he bowled in a
men's league one night a week and did things with
the Indian Guides, which George Q. belonged to, and
the Explorer Scouts with Jonathan. On Sundays he and
Mrs. Cassidy had breakfast together, alone, at a Pan-
cake House near church, and they spent most of the
afternoon in their room while the kids prepared Sunday dinner. By Sunday night he was back to his TV

repair business. He took little time for conversation, though when he talked, everybody listened. In that way he was very unlike his wife, who chattered constantly and was usually tuned out by her kids.

"I can hardly believe we're getting rid of our 1898 kitchen. They made shelves for Amazons then, Watusis. I'm short, of course, below the national average, but I never could reach a thing in these cabinets." That's why, Ruthie figured, quite a few things were usually stacked and piled all over the counters.

Mrs. Cassidy was not much over five feet, and she looked even shorter because a good part of her weight had risen and settled into her bosom. Her coppery hair was always in need of straightening, so she kept it very short. Today she had one of Rita's paisley headbands on, and it made her hair stick out all around her head in different places. She had a perfectly clear complexion, discounting a mass of freckles. The one thing she was careful about, Ruthie always noticed, was keeping lipstick on. Rita said it was really because without it her lips chapped.

"See over there, where Ernie pulled off the old wallpaper? If he'd known it was helping his Dad, I'm sure he'd have picked a different project. Last week he ate his mattress, did you know?"

"Not the Perfect Little Angel? And where is the Angel now?" Ruthie asked. Actually, Ernie was her favorite Cassidy, next to Rita.

"Thank the bountiful Lord for *Sesame Street*. All day on Saturday! Oh, Robert, I just remembered, I've got to take Jonathan to the orthodontist, yes, Saturday at two forty-five. That's today, now. Oh, and I look like a rat. Look at me."

"Just run along, Sweet Potato. I'll take care of things here," Mr. Cassidy replied, measuring wide pieces of wood.

"Thanks, thanks. Just toss Jenny in bed. She's due for her nap. And remind George Q. he needs to get his stuff together for the Guides camp-out tonight." She giggled, pulling the headband off her hair. "Ruthie, ever see a house like this in your life? We could be a TV series. Oh, I just remembered, Rita's not home. She's—where did she say she was going? Honey, watch the oven. Robert? Watch the oven, will you please? The last batch of tollhouses should be done in a minute. Just before you smell them burning, take them out. Nice to visit with you, Ruthie," she called as she flew out of the kitchen door. *"Jonathan!"* She was running up the stairs. "Come brush your teeth at once."

"I guess I'll go up and see Zeke as long as Rita isn't home. Call me if you need help with Jenny or anything, Mr. Cassidy. Here, I'll take the cookies out for you."

"Oh, the cookies. I forgot about the cookies," Mr. Cassidy chuckled.

Ruthie ran up the first flight of stairs, the second

flight a little slower. She pounded on Zeke's door with her fist.

"Come on in," he yelled. He was lying on the floor with his gray bare feet propped up on the bed, which probably hadn't been made since Christmas. He had on jeans, faded nearly white and cut off above his knees. Also a thin T-shirt that was stretched grossly out of shape, like dough rolled out too much. Propped on the slant of his lap was *Playboy*.

"Your room should be declared a national disaster. I'm writing the President about it."

"Aw, come on. It's got that natural, broken-in look, like my nifty cut-offs. I'm almost ashamed to say it, but the room was practically neat this morning, until Jenny the Barfball was up here emptying out my desk drawers. I didn't bother putting the stuff back."

"I noticed. How can you live like this? How do you even find your bed?"

"That's why I keep a sleeping bag in the closet."

"Oh, I don't *believe* it."

"Listen, if you think this is bad, you oughta see my mom's sewing room. If somebody died in there, you wouldn't find him for a week. Did you know we lost a pick-up truck in the garage one year?"

"Your family's really weird, Zeke."

"Except Rita. Man, she's so pure and straight and clear. Her room looks like a mausoleum. Makes me sick to go in it."

Zeke's room was a series of slopes and slants, re-
minders of the attic out of which Mr. Cassidy and
Zeke had carved it. A large burlap sheet hung over one
wall and several unsentimental mementos were fixed
on it with red and black darts. A jock strap was hung
over one of the darts.

"You're probably wondering why I called you up
here," he said, not lifting his eyes from the centerfold.

"No, I just assumed it was because you found me
devastatingly appealing."

"You kidding? I got eyes. I got you up here because
I wanted to find out how the hot romance is going
with Paul Baby." Paul was in Zeke's chemistry class,
and he'd been hanging around with Ruthie lately.
Can't understand some people's taste, Zeke thought.

"Paul Baby has disappeared from my life. No word
for nearly two weeks. You tell me, how's Paul Baby?"

"Cool, great. He cracks the whole chem lab up. He's
so mellow."

"Has he said anything about me?"

"Oh yeah, a word or two."

"Well, *which* words?"

"I just can't remember." He grinned. "Want me to
tell him you're hot for him?"

"Zeke! Don't you dare. I don't like him anymore,
anyway. Hey, guess what. I'm going to be an aunt."

"Big deal. I become a brother every time I turn
around."

"I'd go nuts in a family this big."

"Then you don't have far to go. You're already a paranoid schizophrenic."

"What's a paranoid schizophrenic?"

"It's one of those big college words. You'll learn it when you grow up."

Ruthie tossed a library book onto Zeke's belly. He pulled up his knee just in time. "Please give this to your sister—if it doesn't get lost in the wreck of your late, great room."

"O.K." Zeke moved the book to the floor and was back into the centerfold. He was holding the magazine at various angles to get the different effects of light on it.

"See ya, Cassidy, you big, beautiful hunk of man."

Zeke jumped to his feet in one smooth movement. "Say it again?"

"Forget it. See ya, ugly."

Zeke sighed in feigned resignation. "Well, back to my paper dolls."

Rita balanced Jenny on one hip, feeding her a graham cracker.

"What a slob your sister is," Zeke said, biting into three thicknesses of graham cracker and peanut butter.

"She takes after her big brother Zeke. Look at you. You've got crumbs even in your greasy hair, which incidentally could use a washing."

"I'd sure like to know how you grew up to be Mary

Poppins when the rest of us are all pigs."

"I'm striving to be perfect."

"Oh, barf. Hey, your old pal Ruthie dropped by. I snowed her with the eighth wonder of the world, my room." He scratched under his arm.

"Zekey, I think you like her," Ruthie teased.

"Bellini? Old Spaghetti Body? Are you kidding? She's got as many curves as a Bic pen."

"Curves aren't everything," Rita pouted, smoothing her sweater over her hips. "Ouch, Jenny, you bit my finger."

"Yeah, I gotta admit it, Bellini has you beat, though it's almost a dead heat."


"Listen, Bellini?" Zeke yelled into the phone.

"Oh, no, not you."

"Yea, well, I uh, have a big favor to ask."

"What can I, a mere girl, do for you, Mr. Hefner?"

"Aw, that's just my cover. Inside I'm as soft as a jelly-fish."

"I thought so."

"You did?"

"Just putting you on."

"Sure. Well, um, the reason I'm calling—"

"I'm waiting, Zeke. Why *are* you calling?"

Well, he thought, I'm into it now. If I don't lay it straight, she'll think I like her or something, and she'll think that's why I called her up.

"Listen, Bellini, I've gotta go to this dance, see, that the senior class is throwing. I hate dances, but I'm on the refreshments committee."

"That's appropriate."

"And since I have to go . . ."

"Zeke! Are you asking me to go with you?"

"Well, Rita's already going with some gimpy student-body officer, or something, and so you're my next bet."

"Why, Zeke, that's the warmest invitation I ever had. Before you take it back and invite Lassie instead, I accept."

"That's a relief. I was afraid I'd have to start calling some girls."

"Oh, no, why ask a girl when you can take me?"

"That's kinda the way I looked at it. Thanks, pal. Next Saturday night. Pick you up I guess around eight o'clock."

Rita was standing by the phone when Zeke hung up.

"You asked Ruthie to the dance? I told you, you like her."

"I do not."

"Do too."

"Do not."

"Be careful, or I'll turn George Q. loose on you." George Q. was monitoring their conversation with his leftover Halloween vampire teeth chattering.

Zeke gave him a friendly blow on the head. "You

know, for seven years old, you're really a midget, G.Q."

"I'm telling Ruthie your name's really Ezekiel. She'll never go out with you then, ha, ha, ha," the vampire threatened.

"Shut up, Shorty."

"Ezekiel has a girl friend, Ezekiel has a girl friend," he chanted.

"And you smell like skunk cabbage. Smell him, Rita. Dosen't he smell like skunk cabbage?"

"I don't care," the vampire hissed, "because I'm going to suck your blood." He began munching on his brother's sleeve.

On Saturday night, the fifth of May, Ezekiel Cassidy took a shower. It wasn't his first, but somehow he felt he was giving up something of himself in doing it. Standing in his room wrapped in a thin yellow towel, he flexed his stomach muscles to see if he could release the towel tied around his waist.

"Excellent control, Cassidy. You're a real jock," he told himself.

Then there was the problem of his hair. When he combed it, really took time with it and put goop on it and all, it fell right down around him as if his head were a volley ball. The same if he just shook it dry. And if he put that high-priced men's hairspray on it, the same. It was hopelessly bowl-shaped blond stuff, no matter what he did.

"So what? It's only a crummy dance. And it's only Bellini. It's not like a real date or anything." He tried the towel trick again, surveying what he found under it. "Not bad." He got a mental picture of guys like himself standing in line with towels knotted around their middles compliments of Uncle Sam. "So? That's not the worst thing that could happen to a guy."

He felt jittery when he rang the bell, as if ants were crawling around his chest.

"Why, Cassidy, you washed your face."

"Funny." There was Bellini with her hair piled on top of her head in cheery little curls. I don't believe it, he thought. She has ears. She was wearing blue, a long blue dress with cap sleeves and a waistline clear up under her—she's not a Bic pen.

"What's wrong, Zeke? Have I grown an extra head?"

He swallowed hard. "No, it's definitely not your head."

She laughed, a little too loud, and he stumbled in the door.

"Why, Zeke, you look so handsome."

"Of course I do. It runs in my family."

"Well, maybe handsome's not the right word. Suave just doesn't cut it either. Or *élégant*. No, it's more like —clean."

"Ruthie, look, I'm just thinking," Zeke said, "you

know, we've got to stick it out together all evening."

"Want to call it off now?" she said, hands on her hips.

"No. No, but it seems like the old Cassidy-Bellini number just won't work for tonight, us being so dressed up like movie stars and all."

"I guess you have a point there," she agreed, feeling for a loose pin in her hair. As she lifted her arms, Zeke became even more aware of her feminine endowments.

"So let's start all over, like I'll ring the bell again, and you act like I'm some guy who's taking you out on a date."

"Which you are."

"Yeah, which I am. And I'll act, well, I'll just play it by ear, I guess."

"Is the dance at the school gym, Zeke?" She knew very well it was, but it seemed like a logical way to start things rolling when he had slammed his car door shut and it suddenly seemed they were very alone.

"School gym? You think this is 1956? It's in the Multi-Purpose Room, pal."

Ruthie giggled. "Can't imagine how they'll make it look—oh, you know, all fluffy and romantic."

"I guess they'll hang rosebuds from the basketball nets. I hope the food's good."

"Food! I'll throw up if I eat a thing."

"You nervous?"

"Nervous? No, why?"

"Just wondered."

All the way down by the English Department they could hear the combo. It was loud, full of vibrations carried by the floor. At the entrance to the gym, Ruthie stopped. By magic, it had been transformed into a flowing tent full of color and music and bouncing bodies. But everyone looked different—older, younger. The boys, who had only an hour before peeled cut-offs from their bodies, wore coats and ties—knotted sideways, wrinkled, too long, or tucked into their pants, but *ties,* bobbing to the music and occasionally slapping them in the face when the beat got going.

The girls, who normally wore an endless array of jeans, faded, patched, embroidered, and too long, were ingenues wearing long dresses with empire waists, and chokers around their necks.

Ruthie stole a look at Zeke.

"I like it better for basketball," he responded.

"I don't know, Zeke; it's kind of different. You know any of these people?"

"Never saw them before—not looking like they're going to a funeral like this. Look! Someone's got a taco. Let's go." He yanked her by the arm, steering her between dancing couples as though possessed by hot sauce.

Well, she sighed, he's not Rhett Butler.

Ruthie, who couldn't eat a thing, was into her third taco. She had started keeping a mental chart on the fantastic amount of food Zeke tucked away, but she couldn't keep the count straight in all the different categories. Tacos: six. Cokes: three. Pickles: eight. Olives: anybody's guess.

"How on earth does your mother feed you?"

"Huh?" he answered, wiping hot sauce off his nose. "She doesn't. I feed myself. See?" He devoured the other half of his seventh—or was it his eighth—taco.

"Zeke, how can you eat so much?"

"I like it."

"Your stomach is going to pop if you put any more food in it."

"No, it won't. Not yet. It's seen a lot worse. Want something?" he asked, waving a spoonful of shredded cheese at her.

"Cassidy, I'm getting a message."

"Yeah? What's that?"

"It's that you're busy snarfing down all that food because you can't dance. You can't dance, can you?"

"I can't? Watch this." He pulled Ruthie onto the dance floor with the hand that wasn't holding a taco and began to gyrate and move his overstuffed, skinny body in incredible ways, in rhythm to the music. "Well, don't just stand there catching flies, Bellini. Get it moving," he shouted over the music.

The band needed a break, finally. But the entertainment committee had a stereo on back-up to fill in the silence. That's when a slow, sentimental number somehow got through the amplifier.

"Wanna dance?" he asked.

"Sure," she replied, gaily. But she felt a little funny. He held her at a respectable distance, but even so . . .

Her hair smelled clean, her waist felt very firm. Old Spaghetti Body. Such small fingers in his big, square ones. Her left hand rested lightly on his shoulder, and she didn't move it an inch. He felt stiff, uncomfortable. Maybe he'd feel more natural if he pulled her closer.

She was startled, but she made no effort to pull away. She was going to say something like "You're acting like I'm a girl, Cassidy, watch it." But she thought better of it.

He was a little taller than she had realized, but of course she'd never been up this close to him before. Up against him, in fact. He was sweating on his neck. Maybe he was nervous too. Well, sure he was. His hand seemed so big, and at least, *at least* he didn't have sweaty palms like some guys did—even Paul. Good rhythm. He really feels the music, like me, she thought. She moved her hand to the back of his neck and touched the cold, damp skin lightly.

A shiver ran through him, and he held her even closer. Their faces were together.

She doesn't seem to mind, and it sure feels good like this.

What on earth will I say to him when this music is over?

And so began the whole crazy thing between Ruthie Bellini and Zeke Cassidy. Lunches together at school, snacks after school. They studied together, or rather Ruthie studied while Zeke doodled obscene and crazy pictures and nibbled on whatever wasn't varnished in Ruthie's dining room.

On weekends they went to parties, to movies, to games, to a rock concert now and then. Sometimes they went with other people, but usually alone. Through all the warm months they took long drives by the ocean, stopping to sit on rocks and let the ocean cool them and pull them closer together.

There's no other way to put it: Bellini and Cassidy fell in love. They learned together the answers to the questions their bodies asked, and they echoed and re-sponded fully to each other's needs.

Ruthie felt at peace with herself, for she had some-one to share her warmth and love, someone to laugh with all the time.

Zeke felt enormously happy because he had some-one with whom he could really relax, talk about the things that scared him or made him feel almost like he wanted to cry, without feeling stupid about it. And he loved laughing too. But unlike Ruthie, Zeke was not at peace. He felt restless, directionless. Ruthie had become his world, the bubble in which he lived. Yet he knew it could not be enough for him, and more important, for them.

One day, with a fine, stinging pinprick, he burst the bubble.

"Ruthie, I'm no one. I got lousy grades all through school, barely graduated. I have no burning desire to be an anything."

"You mean like a lawyer, or a salesman, or a farmer?"

"Right. None of those things people want to be. What could I do? Even if I could get into college, which I can't, I'd fall flat on my Cassidy nose. I've got no super mechanical ability. I couldn't stand selling shoes to runny-nosed kids. I'm nothing, Ruthie."

"How can you say that to me? I love you."

"Ruthie, look at me. I just graduated, right? I'm working part-time in a laundry. A crummy eight hundred degrees laundry. I want to get married. But what can I offer you as a husband? I couldn't even keep us in corn flakes. We'd starve in a week."

"I could get a job, Zeke, while I go to college."

"You kidding? You go to school and work, and me sit around wondering what I'm going to do with the next seventy-five years of my life?" He stretched his arms up over his head. "Look at my father. Now, there's what you call a happy man. He works his tail off, but he loves it. He loves everything he does, and he does exactly what he wants, exactly what he does best. He's got a wife he's crazy about too."

"What do you do best, Zeke?"

"What I do best, Ruthie, can't be marketed." He smiled lewdly.

"Besides that, Zeke."

"Nothing, I do nothing best." He stood up out of a cross-legged position and put a record on. Before it even dropped down, he left the room, slamming the door behind him, and went out to the balcony off his parents' room. Ruthie sat on the floor in the clearing of his room and sadly tapped her fingers to the music. About half the record later, he returned.

"I've made a decision, Ruthie. I'm enlisting."

"Oh, Zeke, no."

"It's the best solution. You've heard how the army makes men." He laughed, mirthlessly. "Well, don't you think I'm good material for a man?"

"Oh, Zeke, the *army*?"

"Ruthie, like the posters say, they'll teach me something, a skill, a job, a trade, I don't know, something."

"And you'll have to leave me," she whispered.

He slid down to the floor next to her. "I know."

"Is your mind made up, Zeke?"

"Made up."

"What about your parents," she asked, placing her last hopes in them.

"Oh, my Dad, he was in Korea. He's army through and through. He still goes to Reserves. My Mom, well, as long as I'm not getting shot up, she'll be O.K. with it." He saw Ruthie's eyes fill with tears. "There's no war going on, Ru. I can't get shot in San Antonio or Fresno, or wherever."

"Oh, Zeke," she cried, burying her face in his shirt.

They stood in the afterwind of an earlier 727, 7:15 A.M., Mr. and Mrs. Cassidy, Jenny, Ernie, George Q., Jonathan, and Rita. They stood there pulling their jackets tighter around them, smoothing their hair back against the wind, passing Jenny from one to the next. Ruthie and Zeke stood together, apart from the others, whispering words each would try to recreate when the plane was high in the air and on its way.

"Ruthie, please try to understand."

"I understand." She tightened her arms around his waist.

"When I come home, I'll be a better man."

"O.K."

"I'll have a lot more to offer you as a husband."

She found it so hard to talk. The words kept getting caught in her throat.

"And when I'm out, if you still want to, we'll get married right away."

"Of course I'll still want to. I love you, Zeke."

"Listen, Ruthie, I'll be gone a long time, and there'll be stuff coming up at school. If you want to, if some guy—"

"Oh, I couldn't, Zeke. I'm going to wait for you, right here by this post, until you step back off the plane in three months, or two years, or whenever it is."

He grinned, wrinkling up his whole face. "Hey, I'll send you a picture of me in uniform."

Ruthie remembered a picture of her father in his uniform, looking like no one she ever knew, formal, stiff, unfamiliar.

"O.K., but smile for me in the picture so I'll recognize you." She stood on her tiptoes and kissed his cheek.

"I love you, Ruthie."

"I know," she answered.

"I, uh, gotta go now." They kissed once more, really kissed, and then their bodies reluctantly pulled apart. Ruthie watched as Zeke kissed each of his family, patted George Q. on the head, tickled Jenny's ribs, then walked off to the stairs that fed the plane.

He thought he'd break, he ached so. He felt like a giant cavern, walls all empty and carved out inside. He felt sure the anguish of the moment would never pass, that he'd stay locked in sad loneliness forever. That would never do, not on the first step toward his getting to be a man. So he turned around and called out, "So long, Bellini!"

Stunned for a second, she smiled through a haze of cold tears and yelled back, "See ya, Cassidy."

# JUSTICE

It's so cold. No one has thought to turn up the thermostat against the chill in the house. Byron tosses in his bed, trying to sleep after his ordeal. In the hall, Mrs. Edwards smokes, paces to the front door, back to the phone, puts out a slim cigarette, lights another. Only Jonah is still, waiting for them to come.

He has just shot his father.

The police arrive, three, four, with cameras and an ambulance. Of course, it is too late, so they cover Mr. Edwards and carry him delicately out to the ambulance. So carefully, as though he were still alive. Mrs. Edwards watches, dry-eyed.

"O.K., kid, get your coat. Ma'am, you'll need to come down to the station too," the policeman adds, more gently.

"But I can't. My baby's sleeping."

"My brother. He's six," Jonah explains.

"Ma'am, you see if you can't get a neighbor to come over and look after him. There'll be some officers here awhile. They'll give you a lift when you get things together." He gives Jonah a gentle shove. Mrs. Edwards, who watched as they carried her husband out on the stretcher, can't look now as Jonah walks out the front door.

"O.K., son, from the beginning." He's sitting behind a metal desk, Jonah beside him as if he's being interviewed for a job.

"Name?"

"Jonah Edwards."

"Middle name?"

"Vance."

"Address?"

"Uh, 4119 Kilgalen Road."

"Birthdate?"

"January 5, 1963."

"That makes you—"

"Fourteen, sir."

"Yeah, fourteen. Son, were you informed of your rights when the officer picked you up?"

"Yessir."

"Do you understand them?"

"Yessir, I think so."

"Good. Now tell me, did you shoot your father, son?"

The officer taking notes looks up from his machine to hear the answer, and to watch it.

"Yessir."

"Tell me about it, Jonah."

"Do I get a lawyer?"

"Look, son, the way things are set up in the juvenile justice system, we're all here to protect your rights. Your mother says there's no family lawyer, so we'll have the court appoint one. Meantime"—he wipes sweat off his forehead—"you might as well tell me all about it. Officer Tyre over there is taking it all down, every word, and we'll give it to your lawyer when you get one. It'll look better, son, if you cooperate."

"Yessir."

"O.K., now relax and take it slow. Don't leave out anything." No need to tell him to relax. He looks plenty calm.

Jonah looks at the smudges of ink on his fingers. The ink hadn't washed off after the fingerprinting. He hadn't rubbed too hard, actually. There was a little ink on his shirt, too.

"Well, I came home last night—"

"What time?"

Jonah looks at his watch. It seems like days ago. "About three hours ago, nine o'clock."

"You mean tonight, then, don't you?"

"Yessir."

"Did anybody see you come in?"

"My mother. She was sitting on the front steps."

"O.K., go on."

"Well, I said something to her, I dunno, hello or something, and I went on into the den. I figured maybe Byron would be watching the tube. He, my father, was throwing the kid up against the wall, then kicking him when he fell down. Byron's eyes, he looked so scared and he didn't make a sound while my father was beating the hell out of him."

"Go ahead, son."

"Well, there's a closet in the den. The gun stays up there on a top shelf. I stood up on a camera case and got the gun. I waited till Byron was flat against the wall again, then shot him, my father. It killed him, I guess, but I wasn't thinking about that. I just wanted to get him off Byron."

Lieutenant Olson had been taking behavioral science courses for a degree at the university. He was learning what kinds of sensitive questions you ask a kid like Jonah. "How did you feel about your father, Jonah?"

Jonah's face is quizzical. "I dunno. I never thought about it much."

That's not the kind of answer I'm supposed to get, Lieutenant Olson thinks.

"Did you hate him?"

"No." Jonah rubs his eyes, runs his fingers over a pimple on his nose. "But I sure hated what he did to Byron."

"Did you think about killing him before tonight?"

Jonah thinks for a moment. "I don't remember."

Lieutenant Olson shifts in his chair, shuffles a few papers. He figures he'll try a different route. "Jonah, did your father ever beat you?"

"No, sir."

"What about your brother?"

"He always beat up on Byron, whenever he felt like it."

"And do you know why?"

"I guess he never liked him."

"And what about you, son? Do you like Byron?"

"I guess so. He's just a kid."

"Son, what puzzles me is that if you aren't especially crazy about your brother, why would you shoot your father for roughing him up a little?"

"A guy shouldn't have to get beat up whenever somebody feels like doing it."

"I see." Lieutenant Olson is thinking, this is the craziest case. The kid is so calm, doesn't seem to have any feelings at all about what's been going on. He's guilty as the devil, and he just couldn't care less. Crazy case.

"Jonah, tell me about your mother."

"What do you want to know? She's my mother is all."

"How do you feel about her?"

"I told you. She's my mother."

"What did she do when your father began this, uh, beating of your brother?"

"She acted like it wasn't happening. She'd go outside, like tonight, or upstairs or something."

"Didn't she ever try to stop him?"

"I don't think she ever saw him."

"Do you think she should have done something about it?"

Jonah shrugs his shoulders. Someone knocks at the door. A bushy-haired policeman with glasses puts his head in.

"Lieutenant, the kid's old lady is here."

"Now, then, Mrs. Edwards, I realize this is all pretty hard for you, and we're trying to make it as quick and painless as possible. An officer's with Jonah in the other room, and meantime we'd like to hear, please, what happened when your son came home."

"Byron or Jonah? I had two sons."

"Had, Mrs. Edwards?"

"I said 'have.' "

"Well, let's start with Byron."

"Byron was dropped off by some neighbors. He'd had dinner at their house." She fumbles with the straps on her purse as she speaks. Her hair is limp around her face, dark blond, thin. Her eyes are lifeless also. "My husband," she pauses, stares at a desk calendar, "my husband was in the den watching television when Byron came in. Byron was full of happiness as usual. He was telling us all about what he had for dinner. My husband got a little impatient with him. It was late, way past his bedtime. My husband said, 'Byron, go on up and get ready for bed. We'll be up in a minute to say good night.' "

"And Byron went upstairs?"

"No, no, he didn't. He just stood there, looking at the television. My husband Gerald got really angry and raised his voice." She stops, like she's finished her story.

"And then?"

"What?"

"What happened next?"

"Nothing. Well, I sensed that Gerald was a little angry, and I detest conflicts. So I went outside to let Byron and Gerald work it out alone. I'm too soft on Byron. I spoil him. So I try not to interfere when my husband disciplines him. We waited a long time for Byron, and he's my last baby, you know. My husband always says I spoil him." She folds her hands in her lap.

"Yes, and then what?"

"I sat out on the front steps."

"Mrs. Edwards, did you hear unusual sounds coming from the house, possibly from your son Byron?"

"No."

"Mrs. Edwards, I must ask you this. Was your husband possibly physically abusing Byron?"

"Lieutenant, how can you ask me such a question? Good God, the man isn't even cold yet." She flashes dull anger his way with tired eyes.

"We have reason to believe, Mrs. Edwards, that your husband beat Byron on more than one occasion, and in fact was doing it tonight."

The woman looks incredulous, then she sees. "Oh, Jonah told you that. Lieutenant, my husband is—was a veterinarian. His compassion for small beings is known widely among his clients. Would a gentle man who loves animals and devotes his life to keeping them well beat, abuse, his own small son?" She sits back. She has convinced herself.

Lieutenant Olson clears his throat and flips a few pages of his notebook.

Jonah sits on the narrow bed. There's a washbasin in the room and a mirror, two small chests of drawers, and drapes hung over a fake window to give the room a homey look. Jonah's eyes lazily follow a huge orange and yellow graphic painted on the nubby wall around his room. There's a second bed in the room, but they don't assign roommates to murderers. He's alone, bewildered. He thinks, Tonight I killed my father. I should feel sad, or at least guilty, shouldn't I? I should feel that I, Jonah Edwards, couldn't possibly do such a thing, not to my own father, could I?

But he feels nothing. He lies down, his hands under his head. The door is tall in the room, floor to ceiling. It clicked shut a few moments before with the clattering sound a heavy metal door makes when it locks automatically as it closes. The room is dark. It's after lights-out, and while he hears some stirring, a guitar, faint voices, it is mostly quiet. He stares up at the ceiling until, unaware, he is asleep.

In the morning, there is a warning rattle of keys, then the door opens abruptly. A man in a gray uniform, an older man with a spotty mustache, spits words at him, contempt on his breath.

"Grab your towel, kid. Down to the can."

Jonah stares a moment.

"You. Move it. I don't like saying things twice, you know? Get your butt off that bed and move, boy."

Every morning it's like this.

On the fourth day someone comes with the guard. It's a woman, around forty, tall and lanky, a huge-brimmed yellow hat stuffed onto her head. She wears an orange dress with a sweater over it. The sleeves are pushed up as though she's about to plunge her hands into dishwater. She carries a thin zippered briefcase under her arm. She dismisses the guard with an impatient wave and sits right down on a stool.

"Jonah Edwards, I'm Sara Crownwell. I'm your attorney. I read about you in the papers. You look larger than your picture." She studies him for a moment, head to toe, as though she's memorizing him for a quiz show. "I read about you, like I said, and I asked for you. The least you could do in exchange is be honest. Shall we begin?"

He pulls in, a little frightened. She looks clearly at him, smiles a smile that is warm but disappears as quickly as it came.

"Shall we begin?"

She is new to Jonah, so affirmative. It's as though he's floated for days, perhaps years, and she is an island.

"Jonah, here's what I know about your situation. And incidentally, I still haven't heard your voice. Has it changed yet?"

"What?"

"It's getting there. Well, your case, as I know it." She zips open her briefcase as though she's cracking a whip. She pulls out a few sheets of yellow paper. "You shot your father because he was abusing your brother. Your mother says your father never beat him. And that's the case, period, exclamation point."

"That's what my mother says?"

"Well, now, Jonah, I'm sure you must know that.

Who are you trying to fool? What did she tell you?"

"My mother hasn't been here."

"Oh, I see." There's a sympathy in her voice that irritates Jonah.

"That's all right. I wouldn't expect her. I shot and killed her husband, didn't I? She must be mad as hell at me. I guess that's why she said that stuff about Byron never getting beat up by my father."

"Jonah, I have to consider the possibility that she is telling the truth and you're lying through your teeth."

"What difference does it make anyway?"

"A hell of a lot of difference. It makes the difference between your going free, or rotting in a place like this with doors clicking shut behind you, or being committed to the funny farm. Level with me, Jonah, because you wouldn't like it here for very long, and the other place is a whole lot worse, believe me." She poises her pencil to take notes.

Jonah rubs his thin arms, scratches his neck where the prickly ends of his hair rub it.

"O.K. My father hated Byron, you know, like from the time he was first born. I don't know why. Byron cried a lot when he was a baby, and it drove my father up the wall. He was hitting him before he could even crawl. The bigger he got, the harder my father hit him."

"And you, did he hit you?"

"No. It was like he saved it all up for Byron. Any time he got mad at anybody, my mother, me, maybe even his dumb animals, he'd let Byron have it. I got home one night—you writing this all down?"

"Not all of it."

"I got home one night and found Byron out cold on the kitchen floor. He was bloody and blue and his eyes looked like he was dead."

"Where were your parents?"

"My mother wasn't home. She was out shopping at Penney's or somewhere. My father—"

"Where was your father?"

"He was out in the yard with a goddamn sick tortoise. I made up my mind that if he ever laid a hand on Byron like that again, I'd kill him."

"Jonah, did you say that to the psychologist or anybody?"

"Who's the psychologist?"

"The Sympathetic Ear, the Shrink. Did you mention it to anyone around here?"

"No, I don't think so."

"O.K., this is very important. Very important. You start right now forgetting you ever said that, ever felt it. And I will too. Is that clear?"

He nods. Somehow, he trusts her.


Another time:

"Jonah, I spoke to Byron's teachers at Freemont. They say they've never noticed unusual bruises or cuts on Byron."

"My mother took care of it. She kept him out of school until it all looked clean. She said he had—what does she call it? Oh yeah, chronic croup."

"You ought to know, Jonah, that your mother flatly denies all this. She says your father never once hurt Byron, outside of an ordinary spanking like any kid gets. Like you used to get."

Jonah listens, thinks a moment. "Do you believe her?"

"It's a bunch of crap. But I haven't found the way to crack it yet. She's his mother and must have reasons for handling it all this way." She puts her arm around Jonah, as she jumps down from the stool. She's much taller than he. For a flash, just a fleeting instant, he wants to give in and lay his head on her chest, to be rocked like a baby. But of course he holds himself back.

The setting is formal, modern. A huge walnut desk, small desks on either side of it. A large oval table where Jonah and Sara sit. There is a fence with a gate in it that separates the desks from the rows of benches. On the other side of the aisle sits a small black boy with a full Afro, resting his elbows on his parted knees. A woman, probably his mother, settles into the jelly that is her body, struggling to understand the strange language being spoken up there.

"All rise," they are told as the judge returns. He

wears a dark suit, blue and black tie, no robes, wire-frame glasses. He sits down at the large desk, behind a blue-crockery pitcher of water.

"The February twelfth afternoon session of the Fourth District Juvenile Court of Wyoming County is now in session. Judge Hugh Corning, presiding. Be seated."

The judge pushes the water pitcher away. He mumbles to an aide, "What do we have on tap?"

"Edwards case, alleged murder," the court assistant whispers. "Sitting to the right of the table, Your Honor." She slides some papers toward him. Judge Corning glances up.

"Jonah Edwards, is it?"

Sara pushes him to his feet.

"Yessir."

"Please remain standing as I read you the conditions of this hearing. This is Ms. Crownwell, your attorney?"

She rises also. "Yes, Your Honor."

He begins to drone a memorized, emotionless paragraph about the fact-finding hearing being separate from the dispositional hearing, and something about stipulation and statements, and the words float all around Jonah's head. He touches them, but he can't quite grab them.

The hearing goes on. The superintendent of the juvenile detention home testifies, from the other side of the table. Then Jonah's homeroom teacher. Then the policeman who took him in, and the one who questioned him, Lieutenant Olson, and the psychologist from the detention home. Then his mother comes from the back of the courtroom up to the witness stand. She's sworn in. Sara begins to question her.

"Mrs. Edwards, this whole situation must be terribly painful for you. But it's painful for Jonah as well. Let's try to cooperate and get this over with as expeditiously as we can. Now, then, your description of the events that occurred on the night of your husband's—"

"Murder."

"Mrs. Edwards," says Sara coldly, "this is a hearing, not a lynching."

The prosecutor jumps to his feet. "Objection, Your Honor."

"Sustained. I must caution you to show restraint, Ms. Crownwell. And that goes for you as well, Mrs. Edwards."

"Yes, Your Honor." Sara continues, her tone betraying her annoyance. "We have before us your statement as to what happened that night, so with the Court's permission, I won't ask you to recount the story. However, I have a few specific questions, Mrs. Edwards, regarding your younger son. According to school records, Byron has missed a good deal of school, sometimes for two or three weeks at a time."

"Yes, my son suffers from severe bronchial infections."

"Um . . . hmm."

"They're similar to croup. He becomes very ill, and I keep him home until he's over it."

"Yes. But Dr. Martinette, your son's pediatrician, states that he has not seen Byron since he filled out your son's school health forms nearly two years ago. In fact, Mrs. Edwards, he was surprised to learn you still lived in town."

"Byron's had this, this malady, for many years. I know how to treat my son myself. Don't worry, Miss Crownwell. I take good care of him."

"Oh, I don't doubt that a bit, Mrs. Edwards. And yet, curious fact, the medical examiner attached to this Court, Dr. Jerome Finer, informs me that bronchial infections of the nature you described, severe enough to keep a child out of school for two weeks or better, should be treated with antibiotics, available only by doctor's prescription."

"Just how do you know what I have or haven't given him, Miss Crownwell?"

"Oh, I don't, Mrs. Edwards. And I have no doubt that you are basically a conscientious and loving mother, by your own standards. And because you are, I'm sure you wouldn't want to subject Byron to the ordeal of testifying, himself, in this courtroom."

"Objection! Counsel is threatening the witness."

"Quite right, Mr. Boone. Please, Ms. Crownwell."

"Yes, Your Honor. My point is, Mrs. Edwards, I feel

certain you'll be eager to share the facts surrounding this case with the Court."

"And just what facts are you getting at?" asks Mrs. Edwards. She is swallowing through a dry throat, fighting to stop shivering.

Sara tightens the belt of her wraparound skirt. She casually glances at the witness. "I suggest that Byron has a perfectly fine set of lungs, but that in fact he's had to miss so much school because he needed to recover from blows received at his father's whim." She focuses intently on the woman. "Furthermore, I suggest that you kept him home long after the initial wounds were healed, to be sure that no evidence of the attacks became apparent to outsiders."

Mrs. Edwards turns to the judge and says, in full composure now, "Your Honor, may I say something?"

"You may," he replies, jingling ice cubes in his water glass.

"Your Honor, this woman is making accusations against a dead man, a man who is being disgraced without even the privilege of defending himself. My husband was a gentle caring man. He cherished life and all living things and could not have harmed either of his children. Especially not our baby. He was incapable of that sort of cruelty. I am sure of it. Positive. In fact, if there is such a thing as awareness after death, I feel certain he is forgiving Jonah his death even now."

Jonah holds his head in his hands.

The phone rings, muffled, at the bailiff's desk. He jots down a message and carries it to the judge. Water glass in hand, Judge Corning says, "I'm afraid we'll have to reschedule this session for tomorrow, ladies and gentlemen. Something critical has come up to which I must give my attention. Please step down, Mrs. Edwards." The entire courtroom rises as the judge makes a rapid exit.

Mrs. Edwards leaves the stand and has to pass Jonah's chair. She looks over him and all around him.

"Mother?" He is startled by the high pitch of his voice.

She looks sharply at him.

"Why are you doing this to me?" It is not hurt so much as curiosity in his voice.

"I'm doing only what I must, what is right. You don't see things clearly, as I do, Jonah."

"But how can you betray your own son this way?" Sara asks, pounding a finger impatiently on the table.

"You only see one side of it, Miss Crownwell."

"I would like to see your side as well."

"As if you really could," she says, and she walks through the gate, up the aisle, out of the courtroom.

The lights flood the house, the television is on full volume. Byron, upstairs, sleeps through it all. Mrs. Edwards sits down in front of the TV, takes a bite out of a dry cheese sandwich. Then Sara Crownwell arrives.

"Mrs. Edwards, I have to speak to you."

"Leave me alone."

"I would, but I can't."

"Certainly you can. I'll simply close the door, and you'll go home and forget about being here."

Sara's large brown pumps are planted firmly on the Edwards' welcome mat. "Maybe you can close doors and make things go away. But they go right on existing, Mrs. Edwards." Her voice grows louder, worrying Mrs. Edwards that her neighbors, already too curious with all the publicity, will be poking their heads out their windows. Sara speaks louder still. "But they go right on existing, don't they? Byron has a black eye and bruised ribs, and probably thinks he's garbage the way he's treated. Jonah's penned up at Juvie, lonely and scared to death. And your husband is dead—you're wincing, Mrs. Edwards—dead and sunk ten feet under. How do you feel about hell?"

Mrs. Edwards backs into the hall and Sara follows, slamming the door shut angrily.

"Because if you believe in hell, you can just bet your husband's on a nonstop tour."

"Are you trying to intimidate me?" Mrs. Edwards smiles wryly. "It won't work, because I know that people make their own hell, right here on Earth."

"Why, I would have thought you were a believer. Jonah believes in hell."

Mrs. Edwards shrugs.

"In fact, he's going through it right now. Look, I'm getting to know him pretty well. I see things in his eyes, and I'm not even a mother. Things you see, or would if you looked."

"Why should I look into the eyes of the child I brought into this world, who turned around and felt he had the right to take another life? Not just another life, but his *father's*. You're asking me to look into those eyes to see that hatred?"

"You misread the eyes. It's fear that you'd see, not hatred. You think a kid can live with killing his own father? With his mother's betrayal of him? It's making mincemeat of him inside, Mrs. Edwards."

"This must be your first case. You haven't figured out yet that people who commit murder have some inner strength to get them through it."

"He's got damn little left." Sara paces the room, hands on her hips. "I can't believe Jonah is a boy who could kill in cold blood."

"You're paid to see it that way. You're his lawyer."

"Believe me, for the pittance the county pays me I can see it any way I damn well choose. Jonah could not kill in cold blood."

"Cold blood, hot blood, what's the difference?"

"O.K., tell me, why do you think Jonah shot your husband?"

"I don't know. Anything could go on in the mind of

a teen-ager. He's never been very communicative. How should I know?"

"Did you ask him? Have you got any feeling for the boy?" Sara shakes her head incredulously.

"Of course I have. What do you think I am? He's my first-born child. There has always been a special bond between us, even if we don't talk about it much." She moves behind Sara, says coldly to her back, "But because of him, you see, I have no husband. A son cannot take the place of a husband, can he?"

Sara sinks back into the soft couch to think, then sits up straight-backed on the edge of the tweed cushion.

"But Jonah is incredibly frightened. He's lonely, lost. Oh, at first he was resigned to it all. He felt he was right in doing what he had to do, I guess the way you feel you're right. He didn't have any regrets or fear about it. Then I came along and complicated his life. Now, Mrs. Edwards, he's just plain scared, and he needs you."

"I have nothing to offer him. I'm an empty shell."

"But you're wrong, so wrong."

"Who are you to tell me I'm wrong?"

"You're wrong, Mrs. Edwards. You can offer him his freedom. You can tell the truth, and we can build a case to free Jonah. Why won't you do it? Why won't you?" She scratches beneath the rim of her hat, trying to figure out the answer even as she asks the question.

Mrs. Edwards poises the cigarette in her left hand and supports the elbow with her other hand. Her eyelids hang heavily; she does not blink. She begins to speak, motionless, as though she is the ventriloquist for the dummy within her.

"My husband, Gerald, is dead. Has anyone you loved ever died? I loved him more than anything, and he is dead. Whatever dishonor is brought upon him can never be mended. Do you see that? He can't refute it, or make up for it, or anything. That's what dead means, Miss Crownwell. Now Jonah, he's only fourteen. He has a full life ahead of him. God knows it's not easy, but he can give a few years and be over this."

"But, Mrs. Edwards—"

She continues, not aware of the interruption. "Gerald was always kind to me, so gentle and tender. You know, when we were in college, he had such an indescribable empathy for the lab animals that had to be put to sleep. Can you imagine that? He was known for his compassion and gentleness, for his patience. And Byron is so much like his Daddy."

"Lovely scenario. But here's a cold, hard fact about your cozy little family, Mrs. Edwards. You see where Jonah is, behind bars and possibly going on trial for life? O.K., picture in his place a much older person, your tender, gentle, compassionate, sensitive husband, swinging or frying. Because I'll tell you something sure as hell. Maybe not this month, or even this year, but,

God knows, someday soon, your husband would have killed Byron. Beaten him to death, Mrs. Edwards."

She hears the words, closes her eyes to make them disappear. But inward-turned, they dislodge the demon of fear she's hosted since Byron's infancy. She begins to twist her wedding band fast, faster. "Byron is so much like his daddy, gentle, loving." She cocks her head to the left, emptied of the fear which now fills the room, and speaks calmly. "But he never made Gerald happy. Gerald was always devoted to Jonah, devoted, but he never felt right about Byron." Her face is twisted in painful questioning. "I never could understand it. He was there with me the minute Byron was born. He loved him as immediately and intensely as I did. But—" She pauses, her voice tightens, her eyes open in a dull stare.

"I had a dream once. Of course I never told Gerald about it. It would have upset him terribly. I dreamed that Byron and Gerald were riding a magnificent black stallion along the beach. Mexico, I think it was. Gerald wanted to go faster, but it was very hard for the horse to gallop on the sand. He whipped the stallion until it was in such a frenzy that it madly ran into the water. Gerald jumped off, but Byron was left holding tightly to the horse's reins. Both drowned, the horse and Byron. And I remember his face, Gerald's, watching on the beach. Triumph. No, more than triumph. Almost a look of religious ecstasy. That expression on

Gerald's face haunted me for months, and then finally it was gone. Until now."

Sara waited silently.

"Gerald and I never spoke of his treatment of Byron. He was a strong, prideful man. He would have been terribly hurt if I'd questioned his judgment. I couldn't have talked to him about it. It would have humiliated him. I loved him deeply. Deeply."

She cannot cry, but feeling empty, she crumbles onto the couch, like walls caving in. Sara pats her back gently and whispers, "Jonah's waiting."

Guests usually are not allowed after 8:00 P.M., but a lawyer on official business is admitted at any hour. Still, Jonah is surprised to see the door open so late. His mother, for the first time, comes into his room with Sara. They stand apart like strangers, Jonah and his mother, waiting for Sara to introduce them.

"Jonah, your mother has something terribly important to tell you."

Mrs. Edwards looks at Sara, pleading for a reprieve. Jonah, confused, watches in silence, brushing wisps of hair out of his eyes. Mrs. Edwards tries to speak. The words are clots in her throat. Sara's eyes are fixed firmly on her, encouraging her, but warning her that she cannot retreat. Jonah stares at her also, his face empty, or maybe a little curious.

She remembers him as a boy of three, amazed that he's wet his pants again. Then she sees him lost in the shoulders of a hockey uniform, small, defenseless under so much protection. Tears begin to come, trickling for the years she's closed him out, and other things as well. She touches his shoulder, half expecting the padding still to be there. He squirms, he's uncomfortable, but he's afraid to move away.

"Jonah, Jonah." She moves a small step closer so that her fingers can rest on his shoulder without her having to stretch. "Jonah, please try to believe, after what I've done to you, that I do love you."

He doesn't respond. He's thinking.

She takes her hand back, holds it with the other one.

He looks at his shoulder where her hand had been and closes his eyes for a second.

"Oh, Jonah, how can I have done this to you, to all of us?"

His expression changes; he is trying to understand how.

"Can you forgive your father, Jonah?"

"Why?"

"Because he's dead. Because he loved you. Because he was your father. Because then maybe you could start to forgive me too?"

Jonah glances from Sara to his mother. Sara he can understand. She lays it all out for him to see. But his mother is, always was, a puzzle, because with her so much is hidden.

"Love goes funny sometimes, doesn't it, Jonah?" There is a tired, bitter edge to her voice.

"How's Byron?"

"He's fine. You know Byron always snaps back."

Jonah begins to sense the irony of her statement and looks away.

"Jonah, will you let me try to make it up, to start over?"

He isn't sure what she means. How do you start over when you're already fourteen years old?

The silence unnerves her. She says, more pleadingly, "You and Byron and me? We'll start all over, the three of us."

He stares at her. Where are the freckles? She used to have freckles when he was a kid.

"Jonah, please?" She moves closer, cries silently into his hair. It's a little hard to breathe, surrounded by his mother. He needs space.

"You want me to leave, Jonah?" Sara asks. She's the referee, ready to separate them if one hits below the belt.

He pulls away from his mother. "I don't care. You can stay."

Mrs. Edwards picks up her coat, looks around help-lessly. Sara taps a key on the metal door for the guard to let Mrs. Edwards out, so she can go home to Byron.

# SPRING

The sun reflects on the wall. Purple and pink and lavender. Some orange. Dying at the end of its day. Soon, the moon, but after its splash of light through which people hurry to get someplace, it will die too, at the birth of morning.

And always the beep-beep-beep of the monitor, counting the heartbeats.

There is dying all around me. They take the flowers away before they are wilted. They think they know how I feel. But death is there, in the fallen petals, in their eyes. They wait. I wait. How long?

"Do you know what Daniel did today, Michael?" she asks her husband, knowing he'll never try to guess. He's full of thoughts, work, but some of him listens. He's also reading the mail.

"And what did our prodigy do today, Pidgen?"

"He stacked two sets of blocks up on a chair, one stack for each foot. Then he climbed up, I mean balanced himself like a real acrobat, and got to the marshmallows way up on a high shelf."

"My son has a promising career ahead of him, if not as an acrobat, then at least as a burglar. What else did he do today, Pidgen?"

Could I have remembered that, or did she tell me about it? I can't remember anything before it.

The needle in my arm. My head is tired of staying there, looking for a comfortable spot it hasn't discovered yet on the white pillow. I turn it to the left, to the right.

To the left, a window where the sun forces its way in between the folds of the drapes every morning and now makes its silent exit for the night. It's death again. To the right, a door. It bursts open, forced by the foot of an orderly delivering dinner trays, or by the hip of a nurse whose arms are full of weapons from her arsenal in Central Supply. No one knocks. I am

Room 1297, Bed 1. There is no need to knock.

Nurses whose nights are days forget mine aren't. Doctors whose hours fly in seconds forget that my seconds roll like a giant snowball into minutes of hours of endless days.

They came last night, Michael and Ruth, and will come again tonight, I suppose. They can't forgive me for doing this to them. They've made me their world, though I never asked them to, and now their world is crumbling. I can't control it. If I could, would I have spent my seventeenth birthday here?

They burst in singing "Happy Birthday." He holds the door for her while she backs in with the cake, candles all lit.

"Daniel, darling, Uncle Murray and Aunt Sophie will be here later, but we wanted to have this little celebration for ourselves."

"Yes, just the three of us, son."

"What are we celebrating?"

"Daniel! You know very well it's February twenty-first, and that's your own special day. How well I remember seventeen years ago. You little *mumser*, you. You cost us a whole night's sleep."

"Which we never made up until you were three months old. We thought you'd never start sleeping through the night."

"You didn't both have to get up for the feedings in the middle of the night."

"Daniel, nonsense. You were our joy. Now blow out the candles, like a good boy."

I take a deep breath. The effort is too much, and I am dizzy. She sees; she looks at him. Help, do something, she tells him. He reads her eyes. He blows the candles out.

"Did you make a wish, Daniel?"

"No."

To the left, a window. To the right, the door. Upward, I count squares, and holes in the squares. I play tic-tac-toe on the ceiling. I see football plays up there. The heating vent is one set of goal posts, the sprinkler valve the other. It's hard to keep track of everyone's field position. Suddenly it's a battle between two players who fight to the death. The loser, the one who can't walk off the field, they carry him off on a stretcher, and I quickly flip on the TV.

Downward, I see my feet, lying like a pair of tired swimmers in the sun. In the mornings we swing them over the side of the bed, and I try them on. They seem too big for me now, and they don't get me far. A step or two, to a chair that takes me on a rumbling ride down the corridor. I see eyes everywhere.

Why isn't that guy, a young guy like that, out with some chick?

What's he got, anyway?

He must be a load to lift in and out of bed, tall as he is.

No, haven't you noticed? He's gotten much thinner since he's been here.

Oh, he's the guy in 1297, quiet guy, never talks to anyone.

It's a relief to get back to bed, and to sleep. Tomorrow I do it all over again.

"Daniel, Rabbi Rosen wants to come and see you," she tells me.

My stomach becomes a hard knot, and I'm cold. "Is it that close now?"

She seems shocked. "No, my dear, of course not. Rabbi Rosen hasn't been up since you've been here, is all, and you and he were so close during your confirmation. He just wants to talk to you, darling, like he used to do."

"O.K."

"When's a good time, doll?"

"Well, my days aren't exactly all tied up."

"Yes. Well, Michael will talk to him." She always says "Michael." Never "your father," or "Dad." Strange, too, because she's always made me feel she gave him to me, as her own special personal sacrifice, out of love of course.

Standing there, over the pieces of a bike: "When you were little, you thought I could do just about anything, son. All I had to do was change a light bulb, and you thought I could fix the world itself." He laughs, like he's remembering how it felt to be worshipped. "Now, of course, you're a young man of ten," he hikes up his pants, and the keys and nickels jingle, "and you see your old pop can't even hammer a nail without loosening the plaster and mashing at least two fingers. But, son," he says, arm around the boy, "I can teach you things most fathers can't. I can teach you to feel the earth under you. I can help you understand the world around you, son, because you and I are so much alike. You won't need to make the same mistakes I've made, Daniel. I can spare you that, so you'll have time enough to make your own!"

The feeling is warm, but the boy wonders what the hell his father is talking about. How do you fix my bike, he wonders. That's what he really needs to know.

I travel down the hall, watching a break in the wheel come up with every revolution. A girl, sixteen, fifteen, follows along, but I don't say anything.

"I found out your name is Daniel. But does that mean you're always called that, or do people ever call you Dan?"

"Usually not."

"How about Danny?"

Danny! It sounds so ridiculous. No one but Aunt Sophie uses it.

"No? Then I'll call you Danny."

"I never asked you to call me anything."

"I know that. But I've watched you around here. You're a real crab. You never talk to anyone or even smile. You've got me curious about you. So I've decided to take you on. Once I saw this show on TV about a strange, mysterious patient in a hospital who really kept his mouth zipped, like you, and he turned out to be a prince or something from a small foreign monarchy. Are you a prince?"

"No, hardly a prince."

"Well," she shrugs her shoulders in a floppy way, "it's O.K., because I wouldn't know how to address you as a prince anyway."

I give her a look that clearly says that I think she's stupid, but she acts like she doesn't notice and goes right on.

"Are you an Excellency?"

I sigh and look up at the nurse who is pushing my chair. She is listening with a smile, wondering how I'll answer.

"Why don't you start out calling me 'Your Majesty' and then you can switch to 'Your Highness' when you get to know me better."

The nurse likes my answer, I can tell, but again that dumb girl misses the whole point.

"You know, Your Majesty, I've never met royalty. Mind if I come and sit at your feet sometime?"

I notice she wears a long quilted calico robe. Must be a patient here too.

"Oh, why not. There's not much else to do around here."

"In that case, forget it. I've got plenty of other people to hang out with up here."

"You know what room I'm in?"

"I know, 1297."

"How do you know? Do you do bed checks every night?"

"No, no bed checks. But I see you barreling out of 1297 every morning at this time. Haven't you ever noticed me?"

"No."

"You're terrific for a girl's ego."

"Well, my charm's gotten a little rusty."

"If you ever had any. Oh, and another reason I know about you—"

"Know what?"

"About you being in 1297. You interrupted me, Your Highness. You see, I'm in 1279. Get it? 1297, 1279? And one day they brought me your tray by mistake. Blechh," she said, wrinkling up her freckles, "you're on a rotten diet."

"Not food fit for a king."

"Blechh. Even I do better than you do. Hey, listen,

I have a scrapbook of food that I cut out of magazines. Want to see it sometime?"

"Not particularly."

"O.K., I'll bring it by this afternoon." She stops as quickly as she talks. "Hey, this is as far as I'm supposed to go on foot." She spins around. "See you later, Danny. Oops, sorry. Your Nobleness."

The ceiling is a race track. Dogs run in ellipses around it, urgently. Why do they care if they win or not? A giant bone goes to the winner, I guess, and he races out into the middle of the field and buries it while everybody goes to collect their bets.

"Hey, Danny, Your Majesty."

I pull my eyes down from the dogs to this person in the calico robe. She's got her hair in one thick braid down her back, with a red scarf keeping it together. Not too neatly, either. The hair around her face is shorter, lighter blond than the rest, and she keeps brushing it out of her eyes.

"I brought you something," and she flips a notebook covered with some sort of patchwork fabric onto my belly.

"It's my scrapbook. I told you this morning. Didn't you listen? Come on, open it up and drool."

The title reads HEAVILY SPICED, THICK, RICH FOODS I HAVE KNOWN, by M. L. Buford. I open the first page, but the notebook feels heavy. She scoots a chair over to my bed, then climbs onto the chair and sits on her heels.

"Here, it's my scrapbook; let me show it to you, food by food." The first page is a gigantic pizza. "See the anchovies? Oh, Danny, can't you just taste them?"

"I hate anchovies."

"Well"—she flips the page—"how about a banana split? No? Enchiladas? Oh, wait." She licks her finger and catches up about ten fast pages, then flattens them down to show a chocolate cake with at least six or seven layers. "Now admit it, don't you just love it?"

"If you want to know the truth, I'm getting sick to my stomach."

"Oh." She slams the book shut. "O.K., so food's not your thing. That's all right. I can live with that flaw in your character. Let's see, do you like football?"

"It's O.K."

"I despise football. Hockey?"

"Too cold."

"Agreed, too cold. See, I knew we had something in common." She checks the travel alarm on my bed-side table, putting her face right up to it. It looks like she should be wearing glasses. "Oh, God, I'm supposed to be in R.T. right now. Want to keep the scrapbook? No, you don't. Well, nice talking to you," she says, hopping off the chair. And she's gone.

Nice talking to me. I couldn't have said more than ten words altogether.

The next day. The nurse who pushes me down the hall is shaving me, so it must be Monday or Thursday. She knocks, the calico robe person, and bounces into the room at the same time. For some crazy reason I feel a little embarrassed with the nurse shaving me and all. She finishes quickly and leaves.

"So what's the big deal? Half the world's population grow beards," says M. L. Buford.

"I didn't say anything."

She laughs her crinkly laugh again. "Well, that's true. When did you ever? In fact, I'm not completely convinced you have any vocal cords."

I turn my head, feeling a spot on my left cheek where the nurse missed.

"Hey, Danny, I'm over here," she calls, standing on her tiptoes as if she's looking for me in an airport crowd.

I turn my head back to her, and that's all the encouragement she needs.

"I brought you something." She pulls from behind her back a sculpture of white straws. "I want you to know I sacrificed for this. I collected straws for weeks from my three trays and two snacks a day. Imagine. Weeks of drinking milk from the carton. All that wax. But just look at my incredible creation."

"Beautiful. What is it?"

"Look, I know you didn't really dig the scrapbook,

but I just had to show you this. It's a highly magnified longitudinal cross section of meatloaf digesting. I learned about longitudinal cross sections in biology, and I thought I'd never find a place to use it, until I got this inspiration."

"Meatloaf digesting. Oh, hell."

She just stands there, staring at me. Waiting, I guess. So I say, "What an imagination!"

"You could use some yourself," she snaps. "You want to know something? You have the warmth of a cobra."

At first I'm really mad. But she's still standing there with that thick pigtail over her shoulder, and I figure, well, she's gone to a lot of trouble to be friendly, all those straws, so I could at least try. I used to be O.K. with girls.

"If you're going to bring me personal gifts like digesting meatloaf, I guess I ought to know your name, M. L. Buford."

"Promise you won't laugh?"

"I can pretty well promise that."

"Molly."

"Molly? I never knew a Molly."

"I know. Molly's an old lady's name. But, then," she says, her eyes wide brown circles, "I won't ever fit that description, will I? So I might as well enjoy being the world's youngest living Molly."

"You—you're—?"

"In for life? Yes."

"But you seem so healthy, so bouncy, while I lie here hooked up to things."

"I'm in remission. I'm going home in a couple of days. But I'll be back." She laughs a sort of bitter laugh, the first sound she's made that makes sense to me. "Look, I can see you're tired. I'll come back tomorrow, all right?"

Eyes closed.

"All right, Danny?"

"Sure, come back tomorrow."


"Daniel, you haven't heard a word I've said tonight. Are you feeling all right?"

An incredible question. I lie here like a hunk of meat on a plate, at the mercy of the guy with the fork. I am stiff from lying on my back most of the time. My veins are tired and sore where they poke at me every day. And she asks me if I feel all right.

"Just fine."

"Darling, Michael will be back from New York tomorrow. He called last night and said he has something simply wonderful for you. It sounds expensive. Daniel? Daniel, you're just impossible. I might as well be talking to that water pitcher."

"I'm very tired tonight."

"Oh, yes, of course." She sighs, gathers up her coat, purse, and some candy wrappers.

"You out for your morning stroll, Your Majesty?"

"My morning roll, you mean."

"Danny, come sit by the window with me." We look out, twelve floors below. "Look at all those fossils, Danny."

"Fossils?"

"Yes, those tiny things with the round roofs and windows and doors."

I can't believe it. She means the cars. "Oh, those things."

"What do you suppose that ancient civilization used them for, Professor?"

She brings dumb things out of me. "Hmm. It is my very educated opinion that that ancient civilization was having an energy crisis. And those tanks? The ones with the windows? Well, I believe they were used to hoard fuel."

"But, Professor, they're so small."

"Ah, yes, my child. A very strange civilization. They filled them with eye droppers."

"Oh, that explains it all. You know what? I'm being overtaken by a terrific urge. I feel like finding a giant spatula and smearing the tops of all those cars with peanut butter."

"Don't you ever think about anything but food?"

"Not often."

"Chunky or smooth?"

Later, in the room: my eyes are closed, I'm tired from the expedition to the window.

"Want to hear something sad, Danny?"

"That's just what I need, something sad to cheer me up."

"I'll be exiting exactly as I entered."

"What does that mean, Molly?"

"Intacto. A virgin. Isn't that revolting?"

"Sorry, but I just can't help you out right now."

"Would you, if we'd met at a party or something, instead of here?"

What can I tell her, she asks so seriously. "Oh, sure."

"Well, it's O.K. I'll never know what I'm missing. That's some perverted consolation, anyway."

The slamming of patients' records at the nurses' station fills the quiet. Three bells, pause, two bells. Doctor somebody's code.

"Molly, don't you ever resent it?"

"Day and night."

"Then how do you pull it off so well?"

"I've had more time to work it through than you've had, Danny."

"But I've been lying here for weeks, and I just keep getting madder and madder. I've been cheated. That's what I keep thinking. There's so much stuff I'll never get to do that every guy deserves to do. You know what I mean?"

"I know."

"I spent nearly twelve years in school, and now that it's time to go off to college like everybody does and get away from my—parents, I can't. I've never been out of the country. I've never even seen snow. Hell, everybody sees snow in their lifetime. You ever see snow?"

"Once, when I visited my cousins in St. Louis."

"See? Even you've seen snow."

"So who cares about snow, anyway?"

"I don't know, it just seems important."

"That's *it*, Danny. You've got to decide what's really important."

"Oh, yeah, you've got it all figured out. You know, Molly, sometimes you make me sick. Heh, really smart choice of words."

"Go ahead, Danny, let it out."

"What the hell for?"

She only looks at me, waiting like she always does when she expects me to say something. Sometimes I feel she runs my head.

"I'll never drive across the border, I mean even to see Tijuana. I'll never have another sixteen-ounce sirloin, because the chewing wears me out. *Chewing*, for God's sake! You know, I've never had a dog? I'll never have a wife or kid either."

"And you'll never get bald, lose your teeth, get ripply skin or varicose veins or cataracts. You'll never be senile. You'll never get old. It's amazing what a comfort that's been to me, Danny, about never getting old."

"So what's the difference? I'm old at seventeen, same as a sick old man of ninety."

"But, Danny, people spend their entire lives just growing old. Think how futile it must seem to live all your days only to have them turn into old age. By the time you kick off, you've forgotten the good part, the part when you could move around fast without arthritis-strength Anacin and all."

"And this, what we're doing, is better?"

"I have to believe it. What else have I got?"

"You're lucky you can accept it so well."

"Lucky? Nobody's told me that in a long time."

"I meant—"

"I know. A person's whole vocabulary doesn't have to change just because your world does." She brushed hair away.

"It's like a blind man saying 'I see, I see.'"

"Or one of us saying 'I thought I'd die laughing.'"

"That's different."

"No, Danny, look, after I'm gone and you're gone, *it* still goes on. You know what I mean? You and I have so little to do with it, really. Just specks. The Plan is so much larger than we are."

"For fifteen, you're some philosopher."

"I had to grow up suddenly and figure out things most people spend seventy-five or eighty years figuring out. You do too, Danny, and quickly."

I don't say anything.

"Hey, do you know Walt Whitman?"

"Does he go to your school?"

"No, dummy, the poet Walt Whitman."

"I've never heard of him."

"Didn't you read 'When Lilacs Last in the Dooryard Bloomed' in tenth-grade English?"

"Oh, *that* Walt Whitman." I fake a yawn.

"It's a lovely poem, Danny. It's an elegy."

"That's when you break out in boils when you eat something that's bad for you."

"Not allergy. *Elegy.* A death poem."

I turn away. "I never liked poetry."

As usual, she pays no attention. "He wrote 'Lilacs' after Lincoln was assassinated."

"It must have been a big help to Lincoln."

"It's a death poem—look at me, Danny. It's a death poem, but it's also a life poem. It shows you how life goes on, despite one guy's death. Wait, let me go get it for you." She bounces out of the room.

"Don't do it on my account," I call after her, but she's off down the hall. Poet and philosopher, that's Molly Buford. She's gone a moment or two, and it seems so long. Finally she's back. She hands me a paperback, dog-eared to a page that's speckled with food or sweat, things to remind me she's been there often.

"It's a really long poem, so just read the part I marked, here." She leans over me while I read.

# Spring

*Passing the visions, passing the night,*
*Passing, unloosing the hold of my comrades' hands,*
*Passing the song of the hermit bird and the tallying*
*    song of my soul,*
*Victorious song, death's outlet song, yet varying ever-*
*    altering song,*
*As low and wailing, yet clear the notes, rising and*
*    falling, flooding the night,*
*Sadly sinking and fainting, as warning and warning,*
*    and yet again bursting with joy,*
*Covering the earth and filling the spread of the heaven,*
*As that powerful psalm in the night I heard from*
*    recesses,*
*Passing, I leave thee lilac with heart-shaped leaves,*
*I leave thee there in the dooryard, blooming, returning*
*    with spring.*

She finishes faster than I do. She's probably got it
memorized anyway. She eagerly watches my face for
my reaction. I'm afraid I'll disappoint her, so I read the
poem over a second time while she sits on the edge of
my bed.

"Just think about it, Danny. You don't have to say
anything." She slips quietly out of my room, pulling
the door shut behind her and leaving me with her
book.

After about ten readings, the poem starts to hit me. I
call her room, but she's out. One of her Pollyanna
visits, no doubt, spreading the word like Billy Graham,

until you either see it her way or throw up from so much good cheer.

"Returning with spring," he says. You know, usually you don't think about spring much. It's just something that happens year after year. Here in California there are leaves all year round anyway. But even here, in March the buds on some of the trees crawl out one by one, until they accumulate one day and amaze you with a great burst of green. Sure, it happens every year, and it's going to go on happening every year no matter what you do.

But I won't be here for it.

So when I finally notice that spring happened overnight, last night, outside my window, I'm more surprised by it today than I have been any other year I can remember.

# LIKE A TOY ON THE END OF A STRING

❧

I promise this story is true. It happened the year I spent in graduate school as an adviser in a girls' residence hall. I can never forget the incidents, or the aura of the experience.

We became aware of the stealing only gradually. It started out to be a typical girls' dorm story—delicate washables disappearing from the laundry room as a prank, or perhaps because some huge clod wished she fit into red bikini panties instead of cotton bloomers. But the situation grew worse.

Once it was half a pair of shoes, once the top of a knit suit, another time a toothbrush. All things that could hardly be of much use to anyone but the person who had the other shoe, the bottom of the suit, or the teeth which had originally broken in the toothbrush.

We all became sleuths. "It's an inside job, for sure," someone said.

"Naw, it's the janitor getting his jollies."

"I know. It's part of a vicious plot of the house-mother's to get us to distrust each other, so she can divide and conquer."

"I think it's some kind of initiation rites for Greek Week."

"No, probably a Communist plot, like fluoride."

"It's the Arab Coalition."

"You're all overlooking the obvious and trying to look so super-political. I'm sure the guys in Welham Hall are involved some way. I'm not sure how, but some way."

"I think it's an inside job."

"Yes, it's an inside job."

After much imaginative speculation, we all came to agree that it was about as inside as any job could get. Like maybe it was your own roommate. The thing was, you'd go down the hall for a quick drink of water, and by the time you were back in your little cubbyhole, a box of candy was missing off your desk, or about seven cents in loose change, or your French book.

At first we thought it might be some practical joker among us. You know, just a week or so of harmless pranks. But it went on for four months. And it got more frequent, as many as ten thefts a day on the really bad days. And it got more serious as watches, money, books, valuables of every description, mysteriously vanished with absolutely no clues left behind.

Daily, even hourly, we pooled our information in a corner of the hall or in my room.

"O.K., we know that the thefts have been concentrated in the west wing of the second floor," Jessica announced.

"Oh, swell. There are only thirty girls in that wing, and another thirty in the east wing, not to mention the first and third floors. So we've really narrowed it down," said Marsha, blowing a puff of air out her lips. She had her dark hair wound around enormous rollers. "Let's face it. We're nowhere."

"But," Janet reminded us, "it's more than likely someone on Two West, because it usually happens so fast."

"True," we all nodded.

"And that, in a nutshell, is exactly all the information we have, if even that's accurate," Marsha sighed.

"Except for one thing." They all perked up and focused on me. "I'm beginning to suspect we have a very sick person on our floor."

They nodded again and groaned.

I asked, "Do you know what kleptomania is?"

"Oh, sure," Muriel answered eagerly. "It's when somebody steals a lot, just for the fun of it."

"Not exactly," I said, trying to remember some obscure paragraph on kleptomania in my introductory psych textbook four years before. "I think it also means the person can't help stealing, and if I remember right, in classic cases, he or she doesn't even know he or she is doing it."

"Do you think that's what we have going on here?" Evvy asked, pulling her sweater closer around her.

"It's possible, just possible."

The tension mounted higher every day. Each girl glanced furtively around her, wondering, Is it my roommate? My next-door neighbor? Maybe it's our trusty resident adviser. Maybe it's *me*, and I don't even know it. In short, we were all scared.

"Listen, you all, we've got to lock our doors every single time we leave the room, you hear?" the dorm president informed us at a house meeting one night. Everyone groaned. It would be bothersome and demoralizing, but we all agreed to try it.

So each time one of us went down the hall to sharpen a pencil or visit a friend or use the bathroom, she would slide out her door, lock it, clutch the key, accomplish her mission, unlock the door, lock it from the inside, and then sigh in relief, to be safely back in her own

room. Unless, of course, the thief was her roommate . . .

But if just once someone forgot to lock her door, in
the few seconds she was out of her room, something
disappeared. Someone, somehow, was watching our
every move very carefully, and most incredible of all,
was going unobserved herself.

"It shouldn't be hard to track her down," Jessica
quipped one night. "She'll be the one who flunks out.
Nobody could spend so much time watching everything we do and still go to class and make grades."

Once we all got into the habit of locking our doors,
the thief was temporarily out of business. But not bank-
rupt. She simply began to steal our keys. This extra
step didn't seem to encumber her in the least. Instead,
she very efficiently stepped up her operation.

The most frustrating part was that we never could
find any of the hot items, even though we searched
every cranny of the dorm and grounds. Our clever thief
was either absorbing the goods through her pores or
eating them. A suitcase disappeared one night, an item
both difficult to dispose of and impossible to digest.
Still, we didn't find it.

We had two thorough searches of the dorm, too. The
first search took place after dinner one night, around
the second month. I arrived on the second floor in time
to see a frantic group in a panicky football huddle. The
quarterback stepped forward and all the other girls

followed, not wanting to be left undefended.

"We were all here, right here on the floor. No one left. No one came. Just the eight of us." The other seven heads nodded. "And Annie's new nightgown disappeared, bag and all. Just disappeared. It's got to be one of the eight of us." Sixteen eyes stole looks from one face to the next. Everyone looked innocent and guilty.

"If the nightgown vanished within the last few minutes, it's still got to be on this floor, wouldn't you say? So we'll simply search the floor," I enthusiastically announced.

"Simply search" meant going into every room, every closet, every drawer, of every girl on the floor. It also meant going through every trash basket and every bag of sour laundry, which is very unpleasant right after a dorm dinner of U.S. Government Inspected rejects of the animal kingdom.

No nightgown turned up after all that. We did, however, find the paper bag with the sales slip in it. It was casually tossed in the big trash can in the hall and and was easily uncovered after we dug through the cigarette ashes, french fries with catsup hardened on them, about a ream's worth of the skeleton of a term paper, two beer cans, and a year's accumulation of used end papers from someone's roller bag.

The second search was similar to the first, except we searched every room in the dorm and not just those on Two West. And it took half the night. Still, no stolen goods turned up.

But many suspects did. In fact, just about everyone was a suspect, and everyone's best friend came to me to inform on her. Even George Orwell could not have envisioned so thorough a spy network.

One girl would sneak through the halls when they were empty, rap mousily at my door, and slither in as though my room were a speakeasy.

"I'm *sure* it's Barbara Goote, because she went home last night for the first time all semester, and it also just happens to be the first night we had no thefts."

Or: "It's got to be Linda. I just know it's Linda, because she's the only one who thinks we shouldn't take turns on guard duty all night."

Or: "I think it's Millicent, because she's stopped borrowing money from me, so she must be getting it somewhere else."

But there was one girl most of us suspected, and we were only too eager to pin it on her. "Look, it's perfect. Muriel Stemmons is the dorm busybody. She always knows exactly what we're doing at any given time. I swear, she keeps charts on us all!" Rebecca proudly proclaimed.

"You're right. It's got to be Old Muriel," Marsha agreed.

Muriel was a vision. She was about four feet nine. To say she was plump would be gentle. Her skin was like an ad for acne. She had incurably curly, mouse-gray-brown hair, and she was busty in an old-nanny sort of way. When she went bra-less and ran, the earth rumbled. No one liked her; she smelled. So naturally she was the ideal suspect. It had to be Muriel. In fact, we'd be terribly disappointed if it turned out not to be.

The Muriel situation festered and finally popped one night in January, when a Two West informer brought me a dramatic announcement:

"The Town Crier, and you know who I mean, is pulling a cool one tonight. Would you believe she's marching up and down the halls trying all the door-knobs? That's an out-and-out confession if you ask me. I wouldn't think even Old Muriel would be that stupid."

That was what griped us: If Muriel was such a dolt, how could she have deceived us all so cleverly? We decided she must acquire special mental powers in her periods of madness. Oh, we had it all figured out.

Well, it did look a little suspicious, her trying all the doors. So I decided, at least, to talk to the prime suspect herself.

Before I was even halfway down the hall, the word had spread that an interrogation squad was en route, and the whole wing of girls served as silent observers and potential lynching gang—should one be needed—outside Muriel's door. I swallowed and shook a lot and knocked.

Muriel was very polite and acted as though she had no idea I'd come to question her basic integrity. She must have known, of course.

"Uh, Muriel, were you looking for someone a little while ago? The reason I ask, silly as it seems, is because you were trying doorknobs up and down the hall. At least that's what I hear."

Muriel was sitting with her arms locked behind her back. That was an awesome sight. "Yes, I certainly was. I was making positively sure that every single door was locked tight."

"But Muriel, why is it your concern if everyone's door is locked, or not?"

"Safety. I just had to make sure everyone was safe tonight," she replied.

"Well, that's very thoughtful of you, but, well, people are sort of nervous and suspicious these days, and somebody might get the wrong idea about your maternal protectiveness." I got the feeling I was not approaching the subject with quite enough tact.

"There's something that you ought to know. You see, my butcher knife's been stolen."

"Your *butcher* knife?"

"Shhh! You want them to hear? I brought it from home to cut my birthday cake, but it's gone."

"Oh, come on now, Muriel."

She shook her head firmly, dislodging a few flakes. "No, it's gone. Stolen. And I'm afraid the thief is plan-

ning something unwholesome, violent, you understand? So I was making absolutely sure everyone's
door was locked before I could consider resting for the
night."

"O.K., O.K. But just promise me one thing, Muriel.
Promise you won't tell a single person about this."

"I cross my heart and hope to die," she solemnly
swore, making a huge sweep of her chest, "that I will
not say a word."

Of course by morning at least half the campus knew
about the knife. Some were sure it had been found with
blood still moist on the blade. Others heard it wasn't
exactly a butcher knife—more like a meat cleaver.

"There were voices, men's voices, right outside our
door," Evvy reported. And Cheryl described a weird
shadow with something that looked very much like a
knife, or a dagger, lurking outside her window. So
everyone moved bureaus up against the doors to make
it a little harder for the knifer to get in.

The panic engendered by the missing knife was
enough to lift suspicion from Old Muriel. Eventually,
she found her knife—a large paring knife, not quite of
butcher proportions—in her bathroom locker, where
she'd left it after washing off its three-day growth of
cake. After that, we no longer trembled in fear for our
lives. But the stealing continued.

Finally, in late January, our case had its first real
breakthrough. Evidence pointed quite decidedly to one

girl. Her three closest friends on the floor came to tell me of their growing suspicions, particularly in hopes that I might convince them they were wrong.

"Does Marsha know you're all here talking to me now?" I asked them. I really hated to think of her barging in and finding her finky friends conspiring in my room.

"No, she's down in the Rec Room stealing passages from *Seventeen* for her English notebook."

"Well, she's versatile all right, isn't she?"

"No, really, I'm worried about her," Mary Ann said. "She's such a sweet girl, really."

"And to think that I took her home with me over Thanksgiving," Sally sadly recalled.

"Now wait a moment. What evidence do you actually have?"

"Well," said Barbara, as though she were summing up for the jury, "first, to our knowledge she's never had anything much stolen. Second, she has one of those big furry-ball key rings, suddenly, and Esther Samuels, on Two East, had one like it stolen last week."

"But there could easily be two just alike," I proposed. "I see them all over campus."

"Maybe. But listen to this. You know what Sally said about Marsha's English notebook? Well, it's kind of like a journal, you know, that you write a few lines in every day? Well, we discovered that she borrows it all from magazines."

"In other words, she plagiarizes," Mary Ann interpreted.

"Mmm. Plagiarism is a form of stealing," I said, fitting my thinking right into their case against Marsha.

"But that's not it alone," Barbara continued. "Last night Sally saw her copying things directly from *Redbook* into her English notebook, and she asked Marsha about it."

"What did Marsha say?"

"That's what convinced us. It was so weird. She denied it," Barbara announced, apparently feeling she'd given the jury the clincher.

"I saw her, and while she was doing it, she was denying it," Sally told us. "Can you believe it?"

None of us wanted to.

Marsha might have sensed that the hounds were hot on her trail, for she never left a scent from that time until the end of the semester. So we never had enough proof even to accuse her fairly.

Marsha was a pretty girl, very precise-looking. Her hair was black and shiny, as if it must have come from a bottle, but it didn't. It was always perfectly combed in a fluffy flip. She tended to be a few pounds overweight, but that certainly never stopped her from being very popular with the boys. In fact, she had really more than her share of boy friends. If you really thought about it, you might say she stole boys away from other girls, then innocently wondered how on earth it could have happened. But she was very gentle and sharing with her girl friends, not devious, and she never flaunted her successes with their boy friends. So I suppose they found it a bit harder to resent her. They tended to blame it on the boys.

I met Marsha's mother once, for a moment, and the woman seemed much older than most of the mothers. She wore her hair pulled austerely back off her face in a graying knot. Marsha never mentioned her parents, and I don't think she had any brothers and sisters. Whenever possible, it seemed she went home with girl friends for school holidays.

"Do you know what really kills me about this whole Marsha thing," Sally asked one afternoon in my room. "What really kills me is that she's been such a loyal friend to me, and I'm such a rat. I just can't feel the same toward her as I used to. I'm sure she feels it."

"Think how I feel," Mary Ann said, so quietly we almost couldn't hear her at all. "She's my roommate. I love her like a sister. And now . . . "

In February at the beginning of the second semester, Marsha trapped herself. She left her room on the way to her Spanish class wearing a canary-yellow mohair sweater. It was a little large on her, as though it had been comfortable on a much taller body.

The taller body belonged to Margaret Fulton, on Two East. "Marsha! That's my sweater."

Marsha, looking extremely puzzled, surveyed her chest, her arms, the length of the sweater over her hips. A piece of fluff drifted up to her face, and she gently blew it away.

"Where did you get that sweater?"

"I—don't know."

"What are you doing with my sweater?" Margaret demanded again, hovering over Marsha.

I watched Marsha slide down the wall onto the floor, clutching her books to her chest.

"Oh, my God, no, no, my God, no," she moaned, rolling on the floor with the books held firmly against her. "My God, my God, help me. I'm the one." She was hysterical, tears rushing down her face as she cried over and over, "My God, I'm the one. Oh, my God, my God, my God."

Margaret rocked her, stroking the yellow mohair.

You can check out any TV detective show and find that the mystery is always solved and explained. All the pieces fit together, and you can flip to another station confident that everything is back in order and justice will be done. Our mystery was solved, finally, but never explained. Where were the stolen items? How could Marsha have stashed them away so quickly, so thoroughly, that nothing but the yellow mohair sweater ever turned up? How could she have done what must have taken huge amounts of time and skill and cunning without any of us knowing it? Without her knowing it herself? It was almost as though she were two people who lived on the same block but never knew each other. On that morning in February, they met at last.

As the resident adviser I had access to information from the housemother, so I heard what had happened when Marsha's mother met with the Dean of Women.

"She'll need to leave school," the Dean told Mrs. Buchanan. "The University regrets this decision, but we feel it's essential for Marsha's well-being."

"Oh, I understand fully."

"Mrs. Buchanan, Marsha is very ill. She'll need psychiatric help."

"You've more than fulfilled your responsibility by telling me of the University's decision, and I appreciate your candor and your concern. But what Marsha needs just now, Dean Reed, is a few weeks' rest."

"Mrs. Buchanan, I can't stress this enough. I'm not a psychologist, but—"

"If you'll forgive my interrupting you, I'm sure you're an excellent Dean of Women, but you're quite right. You're not a psychologist. I do sincerely appreciate everything you're trying to do for Marsha, and I apologize for any disturbance she may have caused in the residence hall."

"If it's a question of expense, Mrs. Buchanan, she's

still eligible for free therapy at the University Counseling Center. Or there's a County Mental Health Center closer to your home."

"Dean Reed, I am the girl's only parent, and I alone know what is best for her. Now, if you'll excuse me, Marsha is waiting in the car with my sister, so I really must be on my way. We have a long drive home." She left smoothly and confidently.

When Mrs. Buchanan was gone, Dean Reed wrote at the bottom of her report to our housemother, and presumably on Marsha's permanent records:

*Marsha was removed from school without academic penalty. Psychiatric help was recommended for her, but was declined, on her behalf, by her mother.*

*Dean Eileen Reed*

# ARRIVING AT A PLACE YOU'VE NEVER LEFT

At nine o'clock every morning except Sunday, Hyman Bross took the lid off the pickle barrel, bent straight over until his face was just above it, took a deep breath, and said, "Umh!"

"Papa, every morning you say, 'umh.'"

"So?"

"So what does it mean, 'umh'?" his granddaughter asked.

Hyman Gross did not answer. Hyman Gross never answered questions directly.

"Is the door unlocked?"

"You saw me do it, Papa."

"I saw you go to the door with the key. Who can say, maybe you stopped to grab an onion roll and forgot about the lock. So. Is it unlocked?"

The girl sighed. "Umh," she said.

Hyman Gross checked the lock. "At nine o'clock the delicatessen opens, rain or shine, sleet or snow."

"You know, Papa," the girl said teasingly, "you're a hypocrite."

"What kind of hypocrite? I don't promise nobody something I can't deliver. I don't cheat nobody out of a penny. For $1.95 they get a quarter-pound corned beef, on rye or pumpernickel, whichever, and lean meat too, not fat. Also cole slaw. Where's the hypocrite?"

"It's Saturday, Papa. How come you open the store on *shabbos*?"

"*Shabbos* is *shabbos*. Saturday is something else. Our neighbors don't have *shabbos*."

"So isn't that being hypocritical?" She laughed and wiped her eyes as she minced the onions for the chopped liver.

"Rosalie Schmosalie, if you didn't come here to my store on Saturday, I'd only have a woman who worked and worked and made my customers happy and didn't torment me always with questions."

"Papa, you love it. All day while you're cooking and serving food, your mind is spinning with answers to questions no one's even thought about asking you yet. What would you do without me? Talk to the chicken soup?"

"Without you, Rosalie, I wouldn't even be here. You'd be lighting *yahrzeit* candles in my memory already three years, and your father, God should bless my son, would sell the store, and here would be a laundry with ten washing machines going night and day."

"Oh, Papa, I love you."

"Sure, and why not? Who else would put up with your questions, questions, questions?" The old man smiled under his moustache, pinching Rosalie's cheek with the firm grip only a grandfather is privileged to use. "Your father, believe me, he doesn't have a brain in his head. No wonder already he's bald at forty-five."

"Oh, Papa, not that again."

"He'd let you, a little girl like you, go into the lion's den, you should sell lawn mowers at Montgomery Ward's. Better you should come here. Here I can keep at least an eye on you."

"I'm old enough to work at Ward's, Papa. Sixteen is old enough. They pay $2.50 an hour," she teased.

"Old enough? When you can reach the top shelf of the walk-in freezer, then you'll be old enough."

"Oh, Papa, I'm not going to Ward's," she laughed, "not as long as you're here."

"So."

A young man about nineteen, from the gas station

next door, pushed open the door. His hands jiggled coins in the pockets of his overalls.

"Morning, Mr. G. That you back there, Rosalie?"

Ignoring him, she continued chopping, the onions stinging her eyes.

"What'll it be today, Eddie, a Danish? A piece cheesecake?"

"Aay, Mr. Gross, there you go trying to make a sale again. Jeeze." He laughed and shook his head. "Just a cup a coffee, Mr. G., and this time fill it up to the top, will ya, for the quarter?"

Hyman Gross slid the cup gently across the counter. Eddie turned the sugar container upside down into his cup, watching Hyman watch the sugar flow into the coffee.

Rosalie chopped faster, the flesh on her arms flapping furiously. Her grandfather busied himself at the meat grinder.

"Here's your money, Mr. G."

"Just put it down on the counter, Eddie."

"Un-uh. Come and get it."

Hyman wiped his hand on his apron and rubbed each hand across his bald head. Then he slid the coins off the counter into his hand that had the half-finger missing. The finger had gotten a little too close to the meat grinder one day, and even years later, on damp days, he felt pain in the part of the finger that was no longer there. Now, of course, it was a dry and sunny

August morning, and he felt nothing.

"Did you count it, Mr. G.?"

"No, Eddie. Why should I count?"

"Taking chances, aren't you? Guy could cheat you out of a penny or two."

"Why don't you get out of here," Rosalie yelled from behind the chopping block.

"You better teach your little girl some manners, Pop."

"Just drink your coffee and go, Eddie," Hyman said quietly. He watched to see that the younger man followed his suggestion.

Eddie gulped the last bit of coffee, slid off the stool, and walked out, whistling.

As soon as the door had jingled behind him, Rosalie threw down the battered Romanian food chopper Hyman had brought with him from the old country.

"Papa, Papa, why do you let him do this to you?"

"You've finished the onions?"

"Papa, answer me!"

The old man turned off the meat grinder and pushed the mountain of ground liver down into the bowl. "He doesn't mean any harm, Rosalie."

"Oh, Papa, he's stupid and vicious, and I hate him."

"Rosalie," her grandfather said sternly.

"I hate him, Papa, whether you approve or not. I hate him."

Her grandfather retied his apron. The tie went twice around him, with enough to spare for a good long bow in the front. Still, he was forever retying it. "And what good does it do to hate him, Rosalie? It makes you feel good?"

"It helps."

"Look at you. Your cheeks are red like from scarlet fever. Your eyes are spilling over with tears, and your tiny little hands, they're shaking. This is feeling good?"

"Oh, Papa, why do you have to be so forgiving? So different from everybody else. After all they did to you in the old country!"

The old man went back to the meat grinder. "Heat up the chicken fat, Rosalie, we should fry the onions."

"Hiya, Ed. How's life treating you?"

"Not bad, not bad. Could be better. Fill 'er up?"

"I only got two bucks. Lemme have two bucks' worth," the driver called out his car window. He motioned over to the building next door. "Been over there yet?"

"To the Jew's? Yeah. Man, he tried to gyp me outta my full cup a coffee again."

The driver flashed a youthful smile, revealing two lower teeth missing. "How come you go there then? The Greek's just around the corner."

"Oh, I dunno," he said. "The old man gives me a laugh. Besides, that chick he's got in there—" He cupped both his hands in front of his chest to show what he thought of the girl, while the gas spilled on the ground.

"Hey, that's my dough you're wasting, you bastard. You're as bad as that Jew."

Eddie, grinning, ran his hand over the bristles of his black crew cut.

"Hello, Hyman," Mrs. Freeman called gaily. She pulled a tall cart on wheels behind her. Her legs were bound with Ace bandages and her shoes bulged where the bunions were. "Hot. It's plenty hot out there, Hy. Don't you have your cooler on yet? Oh, hello there, Rosalie."

"Hi, Mrs. Freeman."

The woman pulled her cart up to the meat display case, then parked it, holding her hand inches behind it as if she were prepared to catch a baby just learning to walk. Satisfied that it was safely balanced, she sat down at a table for two.

"Hyman, is the derma fresh today?"

"What do you think, Esther, derma with mold?"

"Hyman, Hyman," she giggled, her layers of flesh shaking. She began to rub her legs.

"So, Esther, what is it today?"

"Today, my veins."

"I mean, Esther, herring? Liver? A few bagels? What?"

"What's a matter, Hyman?" Mrs. Freeman asked,

her knees spread far apart so that she could massage her ankles. "You're a little on edge today, Hy, if you'll pardon me."

Hyman put a slice of coffeecake on a plate. "Here, Esther. Eat and enjoy, on the house."

Mrs. Freeman laughed and resettled her body toward the table. She ate the coffeecake with her fingers, in two bites. "Not bad, Hyman. Yesterday's was a little moister, but for a man, it's not bad. Oy, my veins."

Rosalie wiped her hands and came to sit across from Mrs. Freeman.

"Why the long face, Rosalie, darling? Am I in Gross's Delicatessen or in the funeral parlor, God forbid?" She spat three times over her shoulder.

"Mrs. Freeman, why did you move here to Kenwood?"

"Why?" Mrs. Freeman's body shook again. "Why not?" she laughed.

"I really want to know. Why would you, why would a handful of families settle somewhere like Kenwood, where no one wants us?"

"Who says?"

"Lots of people."

"Who, Rosalie, darling?"

"Oh, that creep Eddie from the gas station was here this morning making Papa look like a fool, just like every day."

"Ah, Eddie. He's a nothing. He's less than a nothing.

And Hyman Gross, for your information, doesn't have what it takes to be a fool." She leaned closer, admonishing with her eyes. "He's your Grampa, Rosalie."

Rosalie sighed and dabbed at a few crumbs on Mrs. Freeman's plate. "Anyway, what made you come to Kenwood?"

"Can I remember that far back? Sure I can! When Sam, that's my husband, may his soul rest in peace, when Sam was a young man—Oh, darling, was he a dapper gentleman, my Sam!—so, when Sam was a young man, he was a traveling hat salesman. He took the train between Kansas City and Oklahoma City, back and forth, selling ladies' hats. Nobody wears hats anymore. But then, in the twenties, did they wear hats! So Sam took the train, and always it stopped in Kenwood, Kansas, for mail. One day the train broke down, and it was four hours till they could fix it. So my husband Sam, he should rest in peace, got off to sell a few hats. What else could he do? And you know what he found out? Besides J.C. Penney's, there wasn't a place in town to buy a hat. Nine thousand people and no hat store."

"Well, what did he do?"

"Ah, what didn't he do, my Sam? He quick came back to Kansas City and bought out the entire line of hats from what he saved. Then he rented an old store on East 24th Street and we moved to Kenwood. It was just Sam and me, no children. We were never blessed."

"Were you happy here?"

"Who knows?" Mrs. Freeman shrugged.

"And what about the rest of them?"

"Who?"

"You know, the others. The Greenburgs and Rosenthals and Goldmans and Isaacses? Those families. Why did they come?"

"Oh, I guess they each had something to come here for." She thought a minute. "Now, Fannie Goldman came to teach at the high school. No, the grade school it was. And her husband Cy, he never did much anyway, a bum, between you and me, so he came with her. The Greenburgs opened the A&P here, first one in the entire county, big, wide aisles. And Dr. Isaacs, well, he liked sick people, but he wasn't crazy for cities. Once Sam and me were here, it was easier for the rest. The Rabbi didn't come till 1960, when he retired from the fancy synagogue in Kansas City. And your Grampa," —again she leaned forward—"a saint, Rosalie, a saint. He started chopping liver right in this building thirty years ago."

Rosalie shook her head slowly, puzzled. "I just don't understand why you all came here and stayed. They don't want us here."

"Tsk, tsk, Rosalie. How many *goyim* come here to Gross's Delicatessen?"

"It's almost all Gentiles. Papa couldn't make a living from our few families."

"Certainly. And the *goyim* love our liver and corned beef and chicken soup. Am I right? Every time there's a wedding or a christening, who doesn't have Hyman's little pastrami sandwiches on round rye? When a *goy* gets the flu, he doesn't come for a quart of Hyman's chicken soup? Even the Racquet Club"—she waved her pinkie in the air—"even the Racquet Club has lox-and-bagel breakfasts twice a year, spring and fall."

"So that means they love us?" Rosalie asked, sliding crumbs off the table onto Mrs. Freeman's empty plate.

"What else could it mean?"

"You're incredible, Mrs. Freeman. Just like Papa." She jumped up, spilling the crumbs back onto the table.

Mrs. Freeman sat for a moment, then slapped her knees together and used them to push herself up.

"Well, maybe a half-pint herring today, Hyman. Is it fresh?"


Rosalie took her lunch hour at two thirty, after the lunch crowd was through. There was a tiny bathroom in the back of the delicatessen. To see in the mirror Rosalie had to stand on her toes. She smoothed her dark hair down the sides of her face, then felt for the rubber band that held her hair at the side of her neck. She stood on her toes again, studying herself in the mirror.

"Brown hair, brown eyes, brown freckles. I'm all one color. At least if I'd had blue eyes." She took off her apron, dusted her sleeveless blouse, and went out the back door into the heat. She could feel the perspiration, cold for a second as the breeze touched her nose, and then she was sticky and damp all over. Fall was only weeks away, but in August in Kansas it seemed as though summer would hang on forever.

Rosalie's school, Kenwood Joint Union High, was across the street. There were two or three cars in the parking lot, but the school, she knew, would be locked up tight until September.

On one side of the delicatessen was a TG&Y Five and Ten. The windows were crowded with bolts of somber fall prints and inflated whales and buckets and shovels, and a few books with titles like *The Grass Is Always Greener* and *1001 Ways to Amuse Your Child* and *Sally Benton, R.N.* Rosalie went into the five-and-ten, but when she heard the tinkly bell that announced to the clerk that a customer was in the store, she changed her mind and walked back out.

Next to the TG&Y was a vet who closed at noon on Saturdays, and next to the vet, Velma's House of Beauty, where Rosalie saw a row of legs. Each one was supporting a *Silver Screen* or *Good Houskeeping,* and above the magazine was a tiny face hanging out of a monstrous chrome dryer. She turned around and walked back past the vet, past TG&Y, past Gross's Delicatessen, and was almost past Linc Johnson's Texaco Station when she heard a whistle. She tensed but did not stop.

"Hi ya, Rosie," Eddie called. He was rubbing some grease off onto his overalls.

Rosalie crossed the street over to the high school side.

"Who the hell does she think she is?" Eddie muttered to himself. He threw a wrench down on the concrete, making a terrible, ear-jarring noise.

At six thirty Hyman Gross put the lid back on the pickle barrel, pulled the red-fringed shade on the door, and turned the key. Aunt Harra, an old black woman who helped out in late afternoons, was washing the big pots and steam table pans. Hyman grabbed a broom and said to it fondly, "When I finish with you, my fine skinny friend, I will be done for another week, thank God."

"Papa, let me sweep for you. You go on home. Aunt Harra and I will clean up."

"Somebody has to pay the woman for her work."

"I can do that for you. Just leave the money in the usual place, and I'll pay her. Now, go on. Go home and soak your feet and have a glass of hot tea, and read your paper."

"I am a little tired tonight. You're sure?"

"Sure, Papa. Out. Go!"

The old man untied his apron, placed some bills under a sugar container, and left. "Good night, Mrs. Wilkes."

"Night, Mistah Gross." Aunt Harra chuckled while

clunking pots around. "That old man never will get it in his head to call me Aunt Harra like everybody else do."

"But he's old enough to be your grandfather, Aunt Harra."

That really delighted the gray-haired old woman, and she began scrubbing again with steel wool. "Why'd he come here anyway, honey?"

"It's hard to explain," Rosalie said, sweeping under the big booth for six.

Aunt Harra clapped two pots together with a resounding bang. "I got time, honey."

"Well, during the Second World War he was in a camp."

"What kinda camp was that?"

"It was a German camp. They put Jews in them during the war," Rosalie explained.

"Oh, seem like I heard about that on the TV. But it sure don't make no sense. What'd they do in that camp of the Germans?"

"Oh, Aunt Harra, terrible things happened in those camps. They starved and beat the Jews, other people too. They did awful experiments on them. And they killed as many as they could, sometimes hundreds of people a day."

"Don't make no sense to me. Mistah Gross always been a nice man."

"And Papa was one of the lucky ones who got out

alive. Six million people didn't, Aunt Harra."

"How 'bout your daddy? He been in the camp too?"

"No, Papa could tell trouble was coming, so he sent my father to America to stay with an uncle—Simon Stern. You know who he was. He worked in a cleaners back then."

"Mistah Stern, he died long time ago. Little tiny man, I recollect. Couldn't hardly see him over the counter at that cleaners. And ooh, what a mighty voice. I'd be out there getting my newspaper now and then. Used to be a stand just out by the cleaners. Old Mistah Stern would be yelling at his customers. Oh yeah, little tiny man, but a mighty voice. 'Bout flew my hat off one time."

Rosalie laughed. "That was Uncle Simon, all right. He took my father in, then Papa too, after the war. My father was only a little boy, six or eight, I guess. He and Papa both worked for MacPherson's, delivering groceries. Papa didn't know a word of English when he started at MacPherson's." Rosalie dipped the mop into the gray water, wringing it out tight. She raced it along the baseboard toward the kitchen.

"These pots is just about done, honey. You want me to help you mop up?"

"No, thanks," Rosalie replied, darting the mop into a corner.

"Well, then," Aunt Harra said as she fixed a hat of brown and orange flowers on her head, "I b'lieve I'll just go on." She stood there a moment. "Mistah Gross leave you some money for me?"

"Oh, of course." Rosalie slipped the bills out from under the sugar container. "Here it is. Have a nice Sunday, Aunt Harra."

The old woman went out the door, holding onto her hat with a bag full of meat bones and muttering, "Life of me, I can't figure why they put Mistah Gross in no camp."

Eddie got off work at the gas station at seven o'clock. Noticing that the light was still on at the delicatessen, he thought he'd go on in for a Seven-Up. He peeked in the window and saw Rosalie mopping under the display case, her rear end up in the air.

Eddie liked that scene, so he decided to watch it instead of going in. But Rosalie quickly finished and turned out the lights, and he couldn't see anything. He knocked on the window. No one came. He figured she was locking up and would be coming out the back door. He'd just wait in the alley between the delicatessen and TG&Y.

She appeared around the building, a white sweater draped around her and a leather shoulder bag hanging over her hip. Eddie stepped into her path, arms folded.

Rosalie caught her breath. "What do *you* want?" she asked, no longer startled.

He walked up close to her, and she instinctively

backed away. The sweater slipped off her shoulders, but she did not take her eyes off Eddie until she tripped on the sweater. Eddie picked it up and handed it to her. She whipped it out of his hands and stuffed it between the strap of her bag and her hip. Eddie was right in front of her, and she continued backing up until she hit the wall of the delicatessen. Then Eddie put an arm around each side of her and himself in front of her, locking her securely in place.

"What do you want?" she asked again.

"You were rude to me in the old man's store. And you didn't pay any attention when I called you, 'round three o'clock today, when you were walking past my station."

"Called me? You whistled like I was a dog."

"Any chick in town would take that for a compliment. How come you don't, huh?"

"Coming from *you*?"

He pressed closer. "You owe me an apology."

"Never."

"Hey, don't you have any respect for your elders?"

"Not when they act like five-year-olds."

"Eddie doesn't like that, baby." His body was up against hers.

"Quit it, Eddie."

"Apologize."

"God, Eddie, who cares?"

"Apologize," he shouted.

"Then will you leave me alone?"

"Apologize," he said, his teeth clenched.

Rosalie began to realize she might be in real danger, and she felt her heart beating faster and the blood rushing to her head. She turned away from Eddie's steady gaze.

"I apologize."

"That's the cheap way, baby. Say the words." He pressed against her breasts.

"What words, for God's sake?"

"Don't talk God to me, you Jew bitch."

Rosalie swallowed hard, trying to stay calm. But his body was pushing her firmly against the brick wall, and she held her head stiffly back, to keep it as far from his face as she could. She felt tears welling up.

"What words? Just tell me what words, Eddie."

He nuzzled her face with his nose. "Does it feel good, baby?"

She closed her eyes. "What words do you want, Eddie?"

"You apologize to me, bitch."

"Okay, I apologize. I'm sorry. I'm *sorry!*" she shouted. "Now get off of me."

"Say it nice, baby."

"How can I? I can hardly breathe."

"Well, here, let me make it easier for you," he said with mocking courtesy. He ripped open her blouse, the buttons like popping kernels on the concrete. "I let a little air in for you. Can you breathe better now?"

Rosalie's face was hot with shame. She pulled the blouse closed, but he shoved her arms back against the brick wall, leaving her exposed.

"Now, how about that apology, straight from the heart." He moved his hands around her, in a burlesqued effort to locate her heart.

In her head she heard, "I'm sorry I'm sorry I'm sorry I'm sorry." She wanted to say it, to get him off of her, so she could breathe, so she could run. Choked with fear and mortification, her lips formed the words, but she could bring no sound to them.

He pushed his hips against her with a jarring thrust. Like the involuntary squeal of a kitten too tightly squeezed, the words exploded from her mouth with the impact of his body against hers.

"I'm sorry, Eddie." Once said, it was easier. "I'm really awfully sorry." She feigned a contriteness felt within her only as an instinct for survival.

A smile of satisfaction spread across his face. He lightly placed his elbows on her shoulders. "Now we're getting someplace, baby."

Rosalie smelled the perspiration under his arms, mixed with the stale odor of automotive oil. For a moment she thought she might vomit. He stared at her, waiting for her to look at him. When finally she forced herself to look at his face, his features softened, as though he were assured he'd made his conquest.

That was when she lifted her knee and swiftly struck a sharp blow between his thighs. He doubled over, moaning and swearing with pain. Rosalie ran down the alley holding the two halves of her blouse tightly across her chest. She ran past the stores, darkened and locked for their Sunday respite, past the manicured lawns with the late summer Kansas sunflowers nearly as tall as she, past the Calvary Baptist Church, on to the block where each doorpost held a small *mezuzah*, symbol of the Jewish home and assurance that she was safe among her own people.

Monday morning, nine o'clock, Velma was doing a manicure on Mrs. Quentin, the real estate lady. Next door, the vet must have overslept, because a woman holding a bulldog like a baby paced outside the Kenwood Kennel and Animal Shelter. At TG&Y, Mrs. Fennel, the clerk, counted spools of embroidery thread, but lost count each time one slipped off the pile.

And Hyman Gross lifted the lid of the pickle barrel, bent down for a whiff of the spicy aroma, and declared, "Umh." But Gross's Delicatessen did not open that morning.

Hyman straightened up from the pickle barrel and reached for his apron tie, only to recall that he had not put his apron on that day. It was the first time, the first Monday morning, since his gall bladder operation in 1968.

He wore a gray sleeveless sweater-vest over his pin-striped shirt. He usually put on the vest in the summer, against the early morning chill. Already he was getting too warm though. Unbuttoning his vest, he gave way to a great stretch that left him dizzy. Then he unlocked the front door, relocking it as he left, and shuffled his feet along the cobblestone sidewalk toward the Texaco station.

A blue station wagon from the Children's Home waited at the pumps, and Eddie was grinning at the driver, proudly showing her how low her oil was.

"Ya take thirty or forty weight, Miz Emerson?"

"Law', I don't know. That's what I depend on you for, Edward."

"I'll just have a look-see," he said, squatting to read the specifications on the inside of her car door. "Looks like thirty, ma'am." Standing up, he saw Hyman Gross, who was waiting beside the Sky Chief pump. Eddie's smile weakened as he reached for a can of oil.

" 'Morning there, Mr. G."

The woman in the car waited patiently, and Hyman himself said nothing. When Mrs. Emerson's car had jerked away, Hyman followed Eddie into the office.

"Well, what can I do for ya, Mr. G?" he asked, his hands in his overall pockets. "I don't serve coffee here, and you sure don't drive a car."

"I'm here, which you know, on account of my Rosalie."

"She sick or something?"

"I am sick, Eddie. You treated my Rosalie like she was not even a person, Eddie, and me, I won't let nobody do such a thing to my Rosalie."

"Hey, now, wait a second, Mr. G. I dunno what she told you, but—"

"She didn't tell me no lies, and be enough of a man, Eddie, not to tell me lies neither."

"We were just fooling around, honest, Mr. Gross. Just hanging around together. She tell you how she just about crippled me for life?"

Hyman pushed his horn-rimmed glasses back up on his nose. He'd lost some weight, and whenever he looked down, they slid. "Every day you come into my store, and you goad me, Eddie. It doesn't work. It doesn't work because to me you're not important enough I should get an ulcer. But Rosalie, that's again altogether a different story."

Eddie sank into the chair behind his desk.

"What is it you got against us, Eddie? What? That we run a good business? That we don't mind nobody's business but our own? We're happy what we do with our lives, and that you can't stand? You're a sad boy, Eddie, a very sad boy."

Eddie played with a handful of paper clips.

"To me, Eddie, I don't want to hurt nobody. I'm a good man, and I think everybody else is a good man too. But you, Eddie, you disappoint me. A sad boy. I only hope you will grow up happier and not so afraid somebody's going to take something away from you." The old man turned and left the office. When he was halfway across the station lot, Eddie ran to the door and shouted, "You really scare me, Mr. G. What does an old Jew like you know?"

Plenty, son, plenty, Hyman Gross said silently to himself.

"What is this? Eleven o'clock and Hyman isn't open yet?" Mrs. Freeman muttered. "I walked all the way down the hill, with my swollen ankles and the bunions, in this heat, and Hyman's still home, I suppose, laying in bed? Whoever heard of it?" She pushed her cart over to TG&Y.

"Mrs. Fennel, tell me, where are the straight pins? I'm hemming a little dress."

Mrs. Fennel, confused as always, motioned to aisle four, then reconsidered. "Aisle three, Mrs. Freeman. Without a doubt, aisle three."

"Mrs. Fennel, it's eleven o'clock, and where is Hyman Gross?"

"Why, I suppose he's next door getting ready for the lunch crowd. It's Monday, isn't it? Kiwanis day at Gross's?"

"But he isn't there. I looked. I knocked. Nobody. Did you happen to see earlier, Mrs. Fennel, did he come or go?"

"Why I—I—no. Well then again, about an hour ago I saw Edith Quentin, the real estate lady, walk by here, done pretty as a picture, straight from Velma's. Her hair was stunning, simply stunning. My eyes just followed her, I couldn't help it. She looked lovely. She went into Mr. Gross's. Mr. Gross himself, as I recall, was waiting at the door. Why, that *is* strange, isn't it?"

"Strange, I should say. Crazy. Just plain crazy. On Kiwanis day, you say, too?"

"My word, what do you make of this?"

"Mrs. Quentin, the real estate lady, you say?"

"Mrs. Quentin it was. Unmistakably. Velma outdid herself this time. The pins, Mrs. Freeman. That'll be fifteen cents, plus tax."

"Oh, of course," laughed the older woman. "With the pain in my legs, I sometimes forget."

Aunt Harra wore her Monday hat, a blue veil with a mock peacock feather. She backed up to the door of Gross's Delicatessen and pushed it with her ample rear. But it did not budge. She rattled the door, and still it did not give. She put on her glasses and looked across the street at the clock tower above the high school.

"Straight up four o'clock. Where is he at? Ain't like him not to be here."

She carefully put her glasses back in her purse. She wasn't about to go around looking like an old lady. She went to the back door, which she also found locked, then returned to the front. She cupped her eyes and looked in through the display window. Not a soul. No lights. Even the Coca-Cola clock was turned off.

What Aunt Harra did not notice was the small black-lettered sign in the window which said: FOR SALE. INQUIRE AT QUENTIN–ROSS REALTORS, KELLOGG 4–9168.

Aunt Harra was puzzled. She glanced at the blurred clock across the street again, then rattled the door once more.

"You don't s'pose they taken Mistah Gross back to that camp of the Germans, do ya?" she asked her reflection in the dark window.

# LOIS RUBY

was born and raised in San Francisco, California. She received a B.A. in English from the University of California at Berkeley and an M.A. in Library Science from California State University at San Jose and has worked as a young adult adviser and librarian. Ms. Ruby explains her special understanding of young people in this way: ". . . as an only child, I went from childhood to adulthood in about 20 minutes. I got the identity crisis, the plunge into commitment, the flight from responsibility, the idealism and zeal and self-awareness that hit most people around 15 when I was 28."

Lois Ruby lives in Wichita, Kansas, with her husband, a clinical psychologist, and her three sons. This is her first book.